TALES FROM
ANOTHER DIMENSION

A Sci-fi Collection

BY ROBBIE SHEERIN

Robbie Sheerin

Print ISBN; 978-1-7379310-3-4

Ebook ISBN; 978-1-7379310-1-0

WWW.Talesfromanotherdimension.com

Published by Silly Lilly Publishing

Introduction

How will HG Wells react when he awakes 200 years in the future on a strange planet, faced with a terrible truth?

Two young brothers make a frightening discovery about the neighbors.

Do robots secretly want to rule us all?

A scientist goes to the extreme in order to change the future of mankind. But is it possible to change our destiny?

Tales From Another Dimension is a strange and fantastical collection of ten short stories. Robbie Sheerin is inspired by classic sci-fi, and invokes frightening twists and turns with each story.

Travel to another dimension and meet strange characters—sometimes human, and at times not so human. They will make you question the solidity of the Earth and mankind. Explore prejudice, fear, imagination, kindness, empathy, and human frailty.

"The Truth Comes in Storms is wonderfully evocative -and the twist caught me completely unawares. Sheerin is a writer to keep an eye on!"- **Rob Yescombe. Writer of the movie "Outside the Wire"**

*These stories are strong echoes of the classic science fiction of the 1950's, and bring back fond memories of the Twilight Zone.-*Noel Chidwick. **Founder and editor of the award winning sci-fi magazine Shoreline of Infinity**

….Sheerin's Sci-if shorts engage the mind and senses with dread and wonder at the same time. What happens on the moon….stays on the moon, even it's from different planets.- **ARZONO Publishing**

"With a voice of clarity and surprise, Robbie Sheerin is well worth the quick and wondrous read each of his stories provides, the insight into our humanity (or inhumanity) they present, and the lasting impression they leave. Indulge and entertain yourself!" - **Jason J. Marchi, author of *Venus Remembered* with Ray Bradbury and the Barnes & Noble recognized bestseller *The Legend of Hobbomock: The Sleeping Giant*.**

Robbie Sheerin's insightful story "The Protector" is a chilling tale that underscores humanity's most troubling shortcomings. At its core, it reminds us that we must remain open-minded and compassionate toward those who are "not like us" or suffer the consequences.....

..."The Future You Imagine, Doctor, Is Not The Future Of The Future" is inventive and imaginative. In my opinion, all tales about our future should be appropriately apocalyptic.They should shake the foundations of our hopes and dreams .....- **Leith MacArthur, author of "The Death of Harry Crow", from The William Snow Series of thrillers.**

Acknowledgments

Dedicated to my beautiful wife, Beckee. Thank you for your endless support. And thank you to my wonderful daughter, Lilly, who made me tell her stories before she went to bed as a little girl. Thank you for your wonderful imagination.

Thank you to all involved in making my dream become a reality.

TABLE OF CONTENTS

THE TRUTH
COMES IN STORMS

Raj grabbed for something to keep him from slipping. His bright yellow raincoat scraped down the metal roof. Suddenly, the noise stopped as he plunged from the building, arms and legs flailing against nothing. Raj crashed on the asphalt thirty feet below. Rain bounced and splashed on his face and motionless body.

***

"Idiotic robots, they won't replace me," mumbled Raj while mopping the floor.

He watched robots moving from machine to machine, suspicious of their metallic bodies. The factory used to be overflowing with loudmouth machinists complaining about management or "the uppers," as they sarcastically called them, with the implication that those in management considered themselves better or above the lowly machinists. They complained about their rights and what they were entitled to. After all, it was them getting dirty, running the machines in the stinking heat. The factory's oil-filled air always clung to their clothes and hair. The breaks were never long enough. The paycheck at the end of the week never seemed to balance correctly on the pay-versus-work scale.

Sure, Raj had his complaints, but at the end of the day, he remained at the factory once all the men were replaced with androids. He was the custodian or janitor of the building. It was his job to perform maintenance on the property, but he was also trained to carry out basic work on the androids, if needed. It was easy stuff, he thought: resetting the android's computers and replacing limbs and eyes that were worn out or damaged. He even replaced their voice boxes—not that they spoke much.

As much of a help as he was to the robots, Raj still hated them. It wasn't the same as having humans around, with their irritating but amusing idiosyncrasies. There were still some non-androids working at the company: the uppers, material guys, and salespeople. No programmer with their robots had ever been able to mimic those chatty, charming salespeople.

The robots were brought in one by one to replace the men. The hatred and resentment felt by the human employees started to erode the mood of the factory like the waves of the ocean chipping away at a shore line. Damage to the robots slowly moved to sabotaging of the machines and the property. What did the uppers expect when they replaced humans with robots? A man who felt like he provided for his family took pride in his trade and work ethic.

Raj had no family, but he understood what it was like for these guys to lose their jobs and struggle to provide for their wives, kids, and in some cases, aging parents. Men lost their jobs as the uppers got bigger and fatter.

Financially, it made sense to have robots. Robots don't need cigarette breaks. They don't need lunch breaks, and they never complained about upper management. They did what they were told—well, not told, but rather: programmed.

Raj never trusted the androids. It was said that the robots were humanoid because it made them less threatening. The world they lived in was built for humans with limbs and fingers. So, it made sense that the robots had the same human features in order to press the buttons, open the doors, and pull the levers of the human world. Their cold metal bodies gave Raj an unnerving feeling. He always found something odd about their eyes. Yes, they looked like eyes, Raj thought, but behind those blue piercing glass spheres, there were silicon chips and transistors controlled by an emotionless motherboard rather than a mushy brain full of thoughts and emotions.

It was late and Raj was used to working ten-hour days. There was a storm that night, and the uppers wanted him to work an extra-long shift and make sure everything ran smoothly. The lights of the factory flickered as the rain and wind howled outside. Technology had advanced at an alarming rate; lithium battery capacities increased monumentally while not giving up their compact size. Computer chips had finally broken the two-nanometer barrier, and even more amazing were their process speeds. They were lightning fast, yet always sustained a low temperature due to various revolutionary materials. Science had made incredible steps, but the computer programs and algorithms would never be able to tame the savage weather. Robots were not the only thing Raj feared.

He was once hit by lightning. He survived, but was left with memory loss. Raj wrapped up in his rain gear and grabbed his flashlight. He strolled through the machine shop and looked at the robots operating in synchronized harmony, like partners on a dance floor. The robots checked and measured parts, and made needed adjustments to the machines as they produced various components. Machines running machines. Everything seemed normal as Raj headed out, with slight hesitation, into the rain and wind.

Raj darted over the puddles and little streams of water that made their way through crevices in the asphalt. Just as he reached the safety of the small overhanging roof, a bolt of lightning cracked in the woods behind him. He glanced at the row of trees. A bright flash exposed the blowing wet leaves and broken branches. He quickly got his key card out and swiped it through the magnetic slot in the door. The door clicked open and in he ran. He slammed the door behind him and shook the water from the surface of his yellow raincoat.

The room had a large thermal-electric generator—TEG—bolted to the floor. This was no old gas-driven generator. The technological beast created electrical energy from fluctuating heat. Most companies had similar devices in case the power stations went down or if the mainline failed.

A metal conduit pipe ran from the top of the generator out the wall to stretch over the courtyard into the main building. As Raj checked coolant levels and cables, he hoped he would never see the day he was replaced. For now, whenever tech failed— and it did — there would always have to be a human to determine the root cause and resolve it.

The wind howled, and rain lashed against the metal roof. Raj looked up at the roof, hoping it wasn't going to rip open. The heavens opened and unleashed a deluge, the rain pounded on the roof like thousands of little rubber hammers trying to get inside. The thought of running back to the main building worried Raj a little. His wet fingers fumbled on the buttons of his jacket while he prepared to face the daunting storm.

He swung open the door to greet a vast array of puddles and streams rushing into rivers he'd have to ford. The door slammed behind him.

He bolted for the main building, key card in hand, until he opened the door and rushed inside.

Raj sighed, relieved to be safe from the rain and wind, never mind the erratic thunder and lightning—until a sudden rumble shook the building. A huge bolt of lightning struck the roof. Everything went black as Raj tumbled to the floor. He lay in the dark as another rumble of thunder hammered the skies outside. He could feel the power vibrate through his chest and covered his ears in hopes of blocking out the nightmarish sounds.

After a few moments, Raj stirred and tried to peer into the darkness, but it was in vain. His eyes had not adjusted and he could not see a thing. He scrambled for his flashlight, but then had a sinking feeling as he realized he had left it in the generator building.

He wondered why the generator had not been activated since power was lost from the main grid. He sat encompassed by darkness, his sight gone but replaced with heightened hearing. Even through the noise of the rain lashing against the roof, he heard the small motors and servos whirling and whining with each of the robots' movements.

Then he saw the small, blue glowing lights of their eyes.

Something was wrong. When power failed, they were preprogrammed to shut down and enter sleep mode. Instead, they had gathered and were standing in a group.

Raj began to feel a little afraid, trapped with one hundred robots that were not following their programming protocols. Maybe the lightning had created a power surge causing a magnetic field that possibly had a negative—even dangerous—effect on the positronic brains of the robots. He needed to find another flashlight and return to the generator building to restore power.

The twenty years working at the factory paid off. Even with his spotty memory and in the dark, Raj began to feel around and get his bearings.

Occasionally, lightning flashed outside, lighting his way for an instant. The large group of blue glowing lights also helped track his progress. He felt his way around the machinery, always detecting with outreached hands that nothing was in front of him. He would occasionally check the group of blue lights. At first, they all seemed to gather together.

The thunder and lightning was moving away now, but rain and wind still battered the building.

Raj's attention was drawn to new movements of metal on the floor, and the little motors of the robots. The group of blue lights was spreading out. It seemed that they had gotten closer to him. As he studied them, he realized the robots were closing in on him. He froze, hoping that the abominable machines would stop coming for him, but they did not!

He needed to act fast. The robots had various ways of detecting their surroundings: sound, movement, heat signatures, and, of course, sight. He considered his location, realizing a metal staircase that accessed an upper walkway around the ceiling was nearby. It was used to maintain lighting and the air duct systems. If he could get up there, he could confuse the robots that were programmed to only move around between the machines, measuring stations and conveyor tracks and not the upper walkway. They would have to navigate the stairs before analyzing the new surroundings of that walkway. Their delay would buy Raj vital time to get out of the building and contact management. Raj knew the robots could not leave the building, and the door he came in from was now too far to reach in time.

Raj groped for the handrail, knowing it was close. He felt the cold metal handrail and grabbed it, guiding himself into the first step. Raj climbed at a much faster pace than he moved on the floor. Stairs were stairs: one after another.

The only thing he needed to be careful about was knowing when he reached the top, but the railing helped. He also had a sense of how high he was by watching the glowing eyes of the robots below, which still gathered to follow him. His plan kept the blue dots stopped beside the stairs, obviously puzzled by the structure of the steps.

Raj had bought a little time, but what next? *Think! Think!*

Some windows opened onto a roof. Getting onto the roof and dropping down to a fire escape, then safely to the ground outside, seemed the best way out. Raj reached one of the windows and glanced at the robots.

To his amazement, a few had ascended the stairs toward him. Raj struggled to open the window. It had been shut for years, and the oil-filled atmosphere had created a crusty, sticky seal around the window and frame, cementing them together.

He rammed the window with his shoulder, not caring if it shattered. After the second attempt, it swung open. Rain and wind blasted Raj in the face. He twisted away, hopelessly trying to avoid getting wet, and glimpsed a sea of blue dots only yards away.

Without hesitation, he got his knee onto the windowsill and pulled himself out and onto the wet roof below. His rubber soles squeaked across the metal roof, which glowed in the illumination cast by the exterior lights.

Raj paused to find his bearings. Where was the fire escape? He would have to drop down six or eight feet to the level below. Raj needed to be certain of his location. Once he started his descent of the wet, sloping roof, there would be no way back up.

Just then both feet flipped into the air, and he crashed onto his back and started sliding towards the edge. Raj grabbed helplessly at the roof. There was nothing to cling to.

His raincoat squelched loudly as it moved down the surface of the metal roof like a rubber squeegee on a shower door. Suddenly, the noise stopped as he fell from the building, arms and legs flailing in midair. Raj landed thirty feet below onto the asphalt. His body lay motionless as the rain bounced and splashed off his face.

***

Raj sensed the heat of the sun on his face. Birds chirped in the trees around him. His body lay frozen and still, unable to see anything.

In the distance, he heard the voices of two men. Their voices got louder and louder until he sensed they were above him.

"Poor fellow. What on Earth happened here?"

Raj blinked at the two voices penetrating the darkness around him. The last thing he remembered was sliding off the roof.

"Why is he outside?" asked a young voice.

Raj heard the conversation but saw only blackness. Worse, he tried saying something, but no sound came out. His lips didn't move. He was totally paralyzed.

"This guy has been through a lot," said an older voice. "He was struck by lightning years ago. He survived, but incredibly, his positronic brain started developing emotions, and he began displaying feelings like fear, happiness, and anger."

What was the man talking about?

"He even showed signs of deep learning and thinking. Truly remarkable. He is one of the most advanced robots we have."

Raj could not believe what they were saying. A robot? *I'm human, you idiots!* He screamed, "I'm human!!" but nothing moved, and no sound came from his mouth.

"Why do you think all the robots are walking around inside?" asked the younger technician.

"I'm not sure. The only thing I can think of, and we can check their data banks, is that anytime the robots have an issue with their programming protocols they are supposed to seek out Raj. He fixes what he can or calls us."

"When the lightning struck the building, they malfunctioned and needed to be reset. Raj is the robot they go to for that, so we will have to check his memory banks, too."

Horror welled inside Raj. How could he correct their false assumptions? He kept yelling that he was human, but nothing came out of his mouth.

The sound of squeaking wheels broke Raj's whirring thoughts.

"Before we move Raj, let's disconnect his power pack," said the technician.

Suddenly, Raj felt air on his bare chest. Fingers prodded along the side of his head.

In the brief moment before the man's fingers found what they sought, his sight flickered in and out. A cart sat beside him, the letters RAJ blazoned on the side. As his mind digested the explanation of the acronym, he heard a buzz beside his ear.

Robotic Automated Janitor. It couldn't be.

Then Raj was gone.

Part 1

THE LAST OF YOUR KIND

The two astronauts slowly lumbered around taking samples from the sand beneath them. One of them chipped small pieces from a rock and collected them in a little case. Other small fragments floated away.

Suddenly, a crumbling noise above one of the astronauts preceded a shower of rocks falling from the sheer cliff beside them.

"Look out!" yelled one of the explorers as he pulled his partner out of the way of the rockslide.

"Wow, that was close," said Mona as Rami held her.

"Well, you know me, I'm here to protect you from all dangers." Rami laughed, but it sounded a bit forced.

"My hero," said Mona rolling her eyes and smirking.

As they returned to collecting samples, they became aware of a figure walking toward them. They dropped their equipment and desperately tried to make their way to their ship. Their suits and the lack of gravity hindered their progress, and the stranger approached.

The stranger stood in front of the two astronauts. He was five feet in height with bright purple hair. His hair was combed over to one side and flat, giving the bizarre impression of being painted on with a brush. His skin was white and looked almost paper thin, exposing his dark veins. Purple lips stood out against pale complexion.

Even more bizarre was that he wore no spacesuit or protective clothing. His shiny shirt looked like viscose and was tucked neatly into his black pants. On the right side of his belt was a small, glowing blue button. His arms hung by his sides, stiff and rigid.

Rami was mesmerized as his jaw hung open, his eyes glaring through his helmet at the strange figure. He could be the first to communicate with another species, a whole new race. This was the discovery of a lifetime that could change the entire theory of life on other planets!

"He—he—has—he has six fingers," whispered Mona nervously struggling to speak as if she had forgotten how to construct a sentence.

Rami looked at the creature's hands, and with amazement looked back at Mona. With apprehension Rami stepped forward.

"Hello … my … name … is … Rami … and … we … are … from …"

"I know where you are from," interrupted the purple-haired stranger. "My name is Chintos."

He spoke in a monotone voice, pronouncing every word clearly and deliberately.

"And what is your name?" he asked, looking directly at the female.

After gathering her nerves Mona replied. "My name is Mona. But tell me, please, how are you able to breathe?"

"Out here in space, in this atmosphere, I do not need to wear an outer shell. I do not breathe like you."

"Where is your ship, your rocket? How did you arrive on the Moon?" Rami asked nervously and with a slight smile, shaking his head in wonder.

"My ship is located in a crater on the far side of the Moon. I would like to take you there. Please do not be afraid."

"Well, wait a minute," Rami said as he stepped between Chintos and Mona. "We aren't going anywhere!"

"Oh, but you are."

Before they could protest, Chintos had drawn a weapon from his back and fired at them. There was no bullet or laser. The projectile was a round button-like tag that stuck to their suits; the tag glowed blue just like the one on the alien's shirt.

The tags suddenly changed from blue to green, and suddenly they were transported aboard Chintos' ship.

Rami and Mona looked around, stunned and confused. They no longer seemed as light as before, their limbs felt like they had filled with water.

Gravity was stronger now, causing them to feel dizzy.

They studied their surroundings. On one side of the room were control panels and screens. On the other side was an insectarium with glass windows for walls. Inside, strange-looking creatures, plants, and other living objects crept around or oozed some sort of disgusting slime.

Chintos pressed a series of illuminated buttons on a nearby control panel. Each one made a bing or buzz sound when pressed.

"I have filled the ship with oxygen. You can now remove your helmets and suits."

Mona and Rami glanced at each other and then back to their host. Rami slowly slid the metal latch over, unlocking his helmet. He paused for a second, wondering if he should trust this stranger. He motioned for Mona to wait.

Rami then turned his helmet as it hissed, releasing pressure, and lifted it off his head. He took a deep breath. It appeared to be safe. He nodded for Mona to remove her helmet.

"Why are we here?" asked Rami.

"You are my guests." Chintos smiled at the still stunned Mona and Rami.

Mona sensed his smile was insincere. The curve of his mouth did not transfer to his cold, emotionless eyes. A female's intuition was rarely wrong.

Chintos left the room through a sliding door. It made a whooshing sound as it opened, leaving Mona and Rami alone in the room.

Rami peered into one of the glass cases and tilted his head, analyzing an odd-looking flower. It was beautiful in a way, with its red stem and black petals. He realized it mirrored his movements, moving from left to right.

Rami frowned. He brought his face closer to the glass, and the flower mimicked his action. Suddenly, a vine shot out from its pistil and made a loud thud as it struck the glass. Rami jumped back. He spun around in embarrassment, checking to see if Mona had seen him jump.

Moments later, the ship shook. Rami and Mona caught their balance by leaning against a nearby wall.

After the tremors subsided, Mona's attention was drawn to one of the glass cases. Her eyes were straining to see its contents like someone trying to read a book without their reading glasses. She watched as little people no taller than five millimeters walked around small streets and lanes. Mona was like a little child again, smiling and being entertained by small pets and vehicles moving around the model town. Her eyes grew larger with excitement. The minute details of the houses, vehicles, and yards were fantastic.

The people, cars, and dogs began to move backward as if time was in reverse. Her smile changed to a frown.

"What happened?" she whispered to herself.

"They are in a constant time loop," a voice said from behind her. Chintos had reentered the room. "It is an experiment I am conducting. It is very revealing."

"Rami, come and look at this." She waved him over.

"Incredible," he said slowly.

To the left of Mona and Rami was a large glass showcase. Inside was dark except for a glowing red ring. It slowly moved from left to right.

"What's in there?" Rami said to Chintos as he observed them from behind.

"Turn the light on. There is a knob above the glass."

Rami reached up and turned the knob on a control panel. A light gradually lit the contents. In the rear of the room was a shadowy figure. Its outlines showed it had four limbs and a head, but it was featureless—no eyes, mouth, nothing. A glowing red collar circled its neck. The figure turned and began to disappear, as its entire rear surface was translucent. The position of the glowing collar was the only way to determine where it was.

"She was very difficult to catch, as you can imagine," Chintos said, smiling.

"Utterly astounding," Rami said, shaking his head. "What is it?"

"She is known as The Unseen. Her species is extremely dangerous and unpredictable."

Mona turned and faced Chintos but kept her distance from him. "Where are you from?"

"I am from the plant Quaestio. It is located in the Verma solar system."

"What do you do on Quaestio? Is there a whole civilization on your planet?"

"I and my fellow Quaestionites are scientists. We seek out and study other beings and civilizations. We study them to learn and understand." Chintos pushed a few buttons on a panel and a planet appeared on a large viewing screen.

"This is my planet." Pointing with his hand, he extended four fingers.

Quaestio was a purple planet surrounded by yellow and red swirling clouds. Off to one side was a minor planet, or the planet's moon.

"I have traveled 309 light revs to arrive in your solar system. That is equivalent to 500 of your lightyears."

"500 lightyears?" Rami blinked in rapid succession, unable to fathom the thought of such a great distance.

"Yes, it may seem like a long way to your species, but not for us. When it comes to experiments, no distance is too long." The side of his mouth curled, giving way to a half-smile. A fake smile.

Rami frowned and pursed his lips. "Are you experimenting on these creatures?"

"Of course."

The Unseen began pounding on the glass, making Mona jump.

Chintos removed a small black box with various buttons from his pocket. He held down a button, and the red collar on the shadow glowed bright. The shadow's hands grabbed the collar and began tugging at it. The creature fell to the ground and started thrashing around in pain.

"What are you doing?" Rami yelled.

"Stop. You're hurting it!"

"She can take a tremendous amount of pain. Trust me, I know." Chintos smiled. It was the only time that his smile seemed real. His eyes closed slightly with a sick, evil joy before he released the button.

Mona and Rami looked at each other with piercing, fiery eyes, like a desperate couple that wanted to escape an awkward dinner party.

"Well, we need to get back to our ship," Mona demanded. "It is critical that we take off in three hours. Our time frame is very small."

"Oh, you will not need to return to your ship."

Mona scratched her ear and frowned.

"And why is that?"

"Because once we teleported onto this ship, I fired an antimatter fusion missile at your home planet. It was an absolutely marvelous sight. The computer recorded it, so you must see! And now you are the last of your kind. Just like all these other creatures."

"WHAT!?" shouted Rami. His face reddened as anger swelled within him.

Chintos reached for his weapon. This time it released a green vapor, causing Rami and Mona to collapse onto the floor.

"THE FUTURE YOU IMAGINE, DOCTOR, IS NOT THE FUTURE OF THE FUTURE."

The caddy placed the golf bag into the car, and Claymore slipped him a folded five-dollar bill. Dr. Claymore, a biophysicist, was always generous when it came to money. He wasn't being showy; he was simply being kind and sharing with the less fortunate.

He made his way up the coast. It was a short drive back to his house in Beverly Hills. The Porsche pulled up to a traffic light, roof down, engine purring. Claymore noticed an old homeless man pushing a beat-up shopping cart. Claymore was familiar with him. He wasn't a tweaker or alcoholic like many of the other homeless people. Claymore saw the human-being in him and wanted to help.

The man's cart was full of treasured belongings, objects he had scavenged from trash barrels and sidewalks: plastic containers, an old radio, clothes, and toys. Oftentimes, he used them to barter with other street folk.

"Hey!" Claymore yelled.

The homeless man stopped and turned to see Claymore. He waved and smiled, revealing uneven and missing teeth.

He approached the Porsche.

"Take this." The doctor handed him five ten-dollar bills. "Get a warm dinner and hot shower, and stay at a motel instead of the shelter tonight."

"Th-th-thanks doc, that's very kind. You-you-you are a good man, Mmmmmr. Claymore. I see your Red Sox are-are-are thhhhhhird in the league."

"Yes, and first place, come October!" Claymore announced confidently, raising one finger with an outstretched arm.

The light turned to green and off he went.

Claymore was a hard worker, but when he wasn't working at the lab, he was socializing with the rich and famous in the clubs and cocktail lounges of Bel Air and Beverly Hills.

***

It was a hot, sticky evening in the Hollywood Hills, and Claymore was excited to get to the lab. He pushed the accelerator to the floor, revving his Porsche to maximum horsepower.

Claymore was a successful man and possessed all the toys that a rich, handsome bachelor could buy. He had built a successful career as a biophysicist through research fundamental in the treatment of cancer and other diseases that saved millions of lives.

His latest discovery was a drug that would eliminate the flu virus. The World Health Organization had funded the project, and various branches of the government also had fingers in the pie. Claymore was never happy about the latter being involved. However, as long as his discoveries could benefit his fellow humans, he would yield to the government's demands.

* * * *

An alien craft orbited thirty-two miles above Earth, between the stratosphere and the mesosphere. Their advanced technology meant the ship was invisible to any of Earth's space-probing instruments.

Two aliens inside the craft looked at a large screen. On it, they saw a bright blue planet with white swirls just above its atmosphere. It seemed out of place in the vast blackness of space.

"Such a strange race of beings, wouldn't you say?" Fen said to the captain.

"Yes, quite. It seems that whenever humans make any advancements in technology or knowledge, they use it to gain power over other humans. We have traveled through time and space and seen their history of gaining knowledge. They are a strange, destructive species."

Fen rubbed his chin with his unusually long fingers. "It appears some people gain riches, others suffer. While some have much, others have little. They create flying machines but then use them to kill. They discover nuclear power but use it for war."

"Do you believe it's time we step in and help these earthlings in some way?"

"Yes." Fen nodded. "Maybe by letting them see their future, they will rethink their beliefs and ideas."

***

Claymore saw the lights of the lab glowing from the dark valley up ahead. Suddenly, his car lost power and the road went dark. Claymore slammed on his brakes, but without the hydraulic braking system's assistance, the Porsche took longer than usual to stop. When it finally did, Claymore sat for a moment to gather his nerves.

Everything was silent except for bugs and insects buzzing in the bushes around him.

A blinding light appeared in the road in front of him, illuminating the Porsche. Claymore got out, shielding his eyes from the brightness. He could feel heat radiating from the light like heat reflecting off a white wall on a hot day.

Then, just like that, the light dimmed, and two figures appeared.

"Doctor Claymore?" one of the figures said.

It was hard to make out the stranger as Clayton's eyes adjusted in the dim roadway.

"Yes. Who wants to know?" he asked, tilting his head inquisitively.

"We need your help, Doctor."

"Is someone hurt? I'm not a doctor of medicine. I'm a scientist."

"Oh, we know who you are. That's why we have chosen you."

"Hey, see here, what's going on?" Claymore pushed his shoulders back and puffed his chest. "Who are you fellas?" His voice deepened with anger.

The figures were now close enough for Claymore to see. He stepped back slightly at the sight. They were both over six-and-a-half feet tall with slicked-back silver hair. Their heads were unusually big, and their hands and fingers were weirdly long. Claymore walked around the car, keeping it between him and them.

"Don't be afraid, Doctor. We will do you no harm. To answer your question, yes, someone is hurt—or, I should say, many people will be hurt. But you may be able to stop that from happening."

The next thing Claymore knew, all three of them were transported to a field. It was daytime, and it seemed like they were no longer in California. It was cold, and the scenery had changed. They were in another state altogether.

Claymore spun around and staggered slightly. "Hey, what is this? Where are we?"

"Doctor, we are not from your planet. We are from another solar system. My name is Lop, and this is my colleague, Fen."

"What?" Claymore exclaimed. "Another planet? Are we on it now? Where are we?"

"You don't recognize the very town you grew up in, Doctor?" Fen asked as they stood in the field, looking down on the little rural town, nestled between small foothills and a winding river cascading through the valley like a blue snake with its head somewhere behind a distant hill.

A moment later, they were transported to another location: a baseball field. A minor league game was in progress. Family and friends were in the stands. A surprised and puzzled look came over Claymore's face, and the whites of his eyes got bigger as he smiled. "Wait a minute, this is my old baseball field! This is my old team."

"Yes, Doctor, and is that not you in the middle, standing on that piece of raised ground?" Lop pointed at a twelve-year-old boy in a dusty uniform and sweaty hat standing on the pitcher's mound.

"Yes," Claymore said in disbelief. He was unable to stop staring at his younger self. "But how . . . how is this possible?"

"Doctor, as I said before, we are from another universe far away. Our technology is more advanced than anything on your planet. We can travel back and forth through time and space. We have brought you back to your childhood. In fact, we have brought you back twenty-five years to 1933."

"But it was 1958. Why? I . . . I don't understand," Claymore said in astonishment, still watching the pitcher.

"We wanted to show you our ability. We wanted you to believe and see for yourself what we can do. This is just a small demonstration of our power. There is another place we wish to take you—the future."

The next thing Claymore realized, they were in a city. There were no shoppers shopping, and no beggars begging. The silence was eerie. Store windows were either caked in dirt or boarded up. Trash floated across the ground, pushed along by a light breeze. Occasionally, a person could be seen running from one side of the street to the other.

"Where are we now?" Claymore asked, looking around at the buildings.

"This is New York City, twenty years in your future," Lop said as they walked along the sidewalk.

"Where is everyone? What happened over the last twenty years?"

"Very soon, Doctor, you will create a drug that will be used to overcome a flu strain, the strain from which all flu viruses originate. Unfortunately, your government will use your work to develop a weapon, but it will mutate after being combined with a certain blood type and causes a devastating virus that will spread at an alarming rate. At first the symptoms will not manifest, and by the time they do, the victims will have spread the virus to many others. It will infiltrate every corner of your planet. Your government and other world leaders will try to contain it. Some won't believe it's real. Only after their families die from the virus will they see how insidious it is, but by then it will be too late. The virus will ravage your world, killing millions."

Claymore's mouth hung open, and he could not take his eyes off Lop as he described the nightmarish future.

"The governments can't stop it?" he asked desperately.

"To stop the spread, cities and towns will implement quarantine tactics. Mass riots will occur in every major city. People will be required to stay home and avoid contact with others. People won't be able to work and will lose their homes. Some won't even be able to feed their families. For a time, the virus will seem to stop spreading. Arrogance will blind people until the virus mutates over and over jumping from species to species. It will become impossible to develop a vaccine. Children won't be able to associate with other children. Schools will implement educational programs through online systems. Parents with young children will be forced to work from home. Those without children will be forced to work with their hands outdoors, in the fields and cities."

"The future you imagine, Doctor, is not the future of the future," Fen added. "Human society is about to take a left turn. Human touch will become taboo and dangerous. Face masks will become a norm with facial features and identities hidden, causing everyone to look the same. Humans will become afraid of each other."

Fen paused as the noise of a car engine drew closer. The three watched as an old, dented Buick clunked past them. Black smoke floated up from the exhaust, filling the air like soot from a chimney.

"No way is this the future," Claymore said defiantly, pointing at the car. "Look at that piece of crap! This ain't no future."

"Doctor, look around you," Fen said. "This is a city of decay. The whole planet suffers from the same condition. Nothing has advanced, and nothing has grown. The factories have closed, the schools have closed, and this world's infrastructure is failing. Humans are in survival mode, working towards a dead-end future. The world's population is depleting. There are fewer births and more deaths."

Claymore took a few steps forward, shaking his head in disbelief. What Lop and Fen were saying was unthinkable. Could this be the future? The human race had always found a way to survive through the most difficult times: the Ice Age, the Great Depression, the Spanish flu, the Black Plague, economic meltdowns, and world wars. Humans had evolved to survive, but had they finally met their match? He was the one who developed the drug. Was this all his fault?

Claymore's thoughts swirled until he developed a headache. With the weight of humankind's fate weighing on his mind, he slumped to the ground, holding his pounding head in his hands. He grabbed a crumpled newspaper that fluttered nearby. The headline on the front page read, "ONE HUNDRED MILLION DIE FROM PANDEMIC."

Claymore's head thumped harder.

"Doctor Claymore, you can change this. This does not have to be humanity's future," Lop said, staring down at the broken man.

"How?" Claymore cried, looking up.

"The drug you are developing cannot be created. You need to make sure your research is not used. Only then can you avoid this future."

"I need to go back now!" Claymore pleaded. He jumped to his feet with renewed energy.

"We have given you the knowledge you need to change your future. You have one attempt at changing your timeline. When fiddling with the laws of time, one must be very careful as to its manipulation. Please be careful to only change what we have told you." Fen said.

Suddenly, he was back at his car in the Hollywood Hills. The Porsche sat on the road, engine running and lights back on.

Claymore looked around for Lop and Fen. He saw no sign of them. For a few moments, Claymore wondered if he had just suffered a hallucination. Maybe it was due to stress from his long hours at the lab. Then he realized he was clutching something in his hand—the newspaper. It was real. Everything was real—Lop, Fen, traveling through time and space, and worst of all, the virus.

A sinking feeling came over him, and his legs began to shake. His entire body felt like jelly, as if his bones had been removed, and he was sinking into himself. He struggled to breathe like the air was being sucked away from him in a vacuum chamber.

He fell to his knees, feeling no pain as he hit the hard asphalt. As his body slumped forward, he held his hands in front of him, preventing his face from smashing into the ground. Claymore rolled onto his back, arms out, and stared up at the stars sprawled across the black canvas of the night sky.

He was a scientist, and scientists solved problems. To change the future, he needed to change the present. Gathering himself, he stood up and got into his car. He slammed it into gear and floored it, racing toward the lab.

He thought about the drug and the years it took to develop. It had been developed to save the lives of people around the world. The eradication of the flu strain could lead to other diseases and viruses being done away with. Inside, he was torn apart. How could he destroy his research?

He glanced down and saw his old Boston Red Sox baseball cap sitting on the passenger seat. It reminded him of playing baseball as a little boy. He imagined a world without that, without families enjoying each other's company. He remembered New York City of the future in decay, a shell of its former self.

He reached the front gate of the lab. Claymore showed his credentials to the guard and was allowed in.

He ran through the main door and raced to the director's office, bursting in without knocking. Jarad Hobbs, stunned at the intrusion, swung back in his chair, dropping cigar ash into his lap.

"What the heck is going on?" he shouted. "You don't know how to knock on a door, chief?"

Jarad Hobbs was the director of the lab; he wasn't a scientist. He was a money guy. Hobbs had a good relationship with Claymore, and they had worked together for many years. Hobbs was the type who didn't care about the science or any problems his scientists encountered; he just wanted results.

"Listen to me. We need to destroy all our research on the new drug. The military cannot get hold of it," Claymore pleaded.

"WHAT?" Hobbs said. "Are you drunk, Claymore?" He stubbed his cigar out in a cigar tray. "That drug is worth billions."

"The government is going to take this drug and militarize it. But if they do, it will become a deadly virus, killing millions. We need to destroy the drug and the research. I've been to the future, and I've seen what will happen. You need to believe me!" Claymore looked like a madman. His hands and face were dirty, his hair wild, and he had holes in the knees of his pants.

Hobbs stood up. With his large stature, he towered over Claymore. "Listen, son, military officials will arrive tomorrow to pick up all the research and data. Any work done in this lab is their property. You know that. Now," Hobbs continued, realizing Claymore was not himself and that he needed to be treated with velvet gloves, "you need to go home, shower, and get some rest. I think you're overworked."

"No, I will not. If you don't help me, I'll do it myself!" Claymore shouted as he stormed out of the office.

Hobbs picked up the phone and dialed security.

Claymore made his way along the corridors and through doorways to his lab. On his table was a box full of papers and charts containing all his research and data. He took the box, along with a metal container full of vials, from a refrigerator.

He approached the door of the lab but then paused. Claymore could hear the guards in the corridor, so rethinking his escape, he hurried out a side exit and ran toward his car.

He fired up the Porsche and raced toward the exit of the parking lot. The guards at the exit waved frantically in an effort to stop the doctor. It was useless.

Claymore smashed through the barrier, sending wood splinters and glass from his headlights across the road.

Not far behind Claymore were Hobbs and the head of security. A military vehicle had also joined the pursuit. The two cars raced after the Porsche.

Claymore struggled to see in the dark with only one headlight guiding the way. The winding road curved around the hills. The bright lights of the two pursuing vehicles gained on Claymore's crippled car. He forced the car along the dark roads, his vision hampered. His palms sweated as he occasionally lost his grip on the steering wheel. The lights of the cars behind caused his mirror to shine brightly, but he couldn't determine how close they were.

Suddenly, a bend in the road came, surprising Claymore. He tried to turn, but it was too late. The Porsche careened off the road and through the bushes and trees.

The Porsche landed with an almighty crash and began rolling and tumbling down the hillside. Branches of pine trees snapped like uncooked spaghetti as the car barreled to the bottom of the ravine. The car finally came to rest near a campsite.

Moments later, the Porsche exploded into a fireball, lighting up the dark valley.

The following morning, Hobbs and government officials stood on the hill, looking down at the wreckage below. The burned-out Porsche still smoldered as emergency crews and military personnel swarmed the scene like an army of ants.

One of the men near the wreckage spoke into his radio. His voice came through on a radio in Hobbs' hand.

"Sir, I'm afraid everything has been destroyed"

"Damn! Johnson, are you sure?" Hobbs said angrily. "What about the samples?"

"No, I'm sorry, they have all been destroyed, there are no traces of the chemical solution."

***

A large rat scurried around in the undergrowth looking for discarded scraps of food from the campsite. There were always treasures to be found: a banana peel, a half-eaten sandwich, or crumbs from a small child's lunch box.

The rat stopped in some charred grass from a crash the week before. It scratched and sniffed at a broken glass tube; the rodent's whiskers twitched frantically. The grass and seeds that lay around it had been stained purple from the contents of the tubes. The seeds tasted sweet as the rat filled its already bloated belly.

Days later, the rodent journeyed through the maze of sewage systems and down into the city—always eating along the way, as rats do.

The rat's black eyes seemed to bulge out at the sight of the biggest meal it had ever seen. There, laying in the cart of an old homeless man, was a half-eaten burger and potato chips. The rodent had just begun feeding when the old man slammed a stick down, scaring the rat and causing it to scurry away.

Small purple droppings from the rat lay in the cart. The old man brushed the strange purple lumps off of his food, not knowing what they were. He finished eating the burger and potato chips.

It was getting late, and it was almost time to call it a night at the homeless shelter. The old man felt ill, with hot and cold sweats taking hold of his body. He tossed and turned like a soldier tormented by memories of war, unable to find sleep as something insidiously took command of his inner organs.

That night he became Patient Zero and created an unavoidable destiny for mankind.

PROTECTOR

The moon sat low in the sky, its light shining through cracks in the clouds. The ocean beyond the dark beach reflected glimmers of moonlight, exposing its restless and turbulent waves.

Methusel stood on the beach in his robe, his arms outstretched toward the heavens as the sand engulfed his bare feet. His long beard, bracelets, and feathered necklaces blew in the soft constant breeze.

Large sticks protruded from the sand, lining the beach like a barrier between land and sea—a fence with no wire. The skins of dead rabbits, squirrels, and other small creatures hung like morbid tribal flags.

The old man had lived on the beach for many years, until his ancient tent became part of the landscape.

Sturdy pegs and ropes looked like they had grown out of the ground. Grass and weeds encroached on its exterior.

It was rare for people to visit this area, as it was a few miles from any roads and there were plenty of more accessible beaches. Occasionally, campers would stroll out of the trees and spot Methusel. They would curiously watch him from afar or peep out from the cover of the tree line. The recluse had become a legend in these parts. Human interaction with him was scarce, and therefore he was not viewed as a threat.

Sometimes egged on by curiosity, hikers or wanderers would try—unsuccessfully—to talk to him. Hospitality was not a quality he possessed. His words were few and his manners were even less; he mumbled and babbled about the ocean and the darkness. It was crazy talk.

His black skin was weather-worn due to his outdoor lifestyle. His bald head was a canvas of spattered symbols and shapes, strange and unique tattoos.

At night, Methusal warmed himself by a large fire he used to roast rabbits or squirrels he snared. Being carful to salvaged their hides for placement on his flag poles.

The fire was more than just a tool of survival. Methusal burned the animal fat along with sweet incense. The fragrant smoke spiraled high into the darkness above like a gift to the gods.

The peculiar actions and rituals seemed to be of great importance to the priest. His whole purpose for living seemed to be focused on his strange and enigmatic ways, as if he knew something that no one else was aware of—something dark mimicked by his flag poles and mysterious fire rituals.

A few miles from the beach, a disturbance in the woods caused the birds to fly from the trees.

"Come on, fatso, move it!" Mickey mockingly said to Arthur.

Arthur pushed his red floppy hair, which refused to stay in one place, away from his face. He then waddled up to Mickey and shoved him.

"Hey, who are you calling fatso?!" His flushed face matched his freckles.

Mickey laughed and reached out to a tree for balance.

"You! What are you gonna do about it? Eat me to death?"

"Cut it out, idiots. We're almost there." Mary glowered in their direction before stomping through thick undergrowth in her big boots. Boots worn by boys, or tomboys such as herself.

"Why did you bring him along anyway, Mary? He's only gonna slow us down." Mickey pointed his thumb at Arthur.

Mary stopped and turned quickly. "Because he is my friend! He is there when it counts and that's what friends do. It doesn't matter how people look. It's about who they are on the inside."

"Ugh not for me." Mickey dismissively waved his hand at Mary. "My dad says it's about how you look and present yourself. Look at me: lean, strong, and confident." He flexed his adolescent muscles. "This is all you need to get by in life."

"Just because you're my cousin doesn't mean I won't whack you in the mouth. Now leave Arthur alone."

The three of them broke from the tree line and spread out on the grassy stretch. Beyond this point, the ground transformed into dunes which slowly descended toward the ocean. They plowed up one of the dunes and the two boys laid down on the summit, hoping to scope out their target.

"There it is!" Arthur pointed out the small tent-shaped mound in the distance.

"Why are you whispering, fatso? He can't hear us."

"Shut up Mickey! You don't know that."

Mary laid between them. Annoyed by their constant bickering, she elbowed the boys' arms, hoping sore arms would cause them to stop bickering like a pair of old women.

Stories about the strange man living on the beach with his death poles abounded. The kids wanted to see if the tales were true, or if they were the schoolyard gossip of imaginative pre-teens.

They slithered along the beach. Their pace slowed as they approached the first pole.

Mickey tilted his head, studying the blood-stained fur pinned to the pole. It was speckled with grains of sand whipped up from the beach. A familiar scent came from the dead animal.

Arthur pushed Mickey aside. "Wow! It's a ferret!" He sniffed the carcass like a wild animal smelling its pray. To his surprise, it had a vague smell of mint.

"It looks like there are more up ahead," Mary said, peering along the beach.

They headed toward the tent. They became immune to the grotesque poles as they passed them in succession along the beach.

Nearing the tent, they could see a figure sitting by a smoldering fire.

The robe that hung from Methusel made him appear big. But he was skinny due to his diet of rabbits, berries, and vegetation.

Mickey led the way as always, but with caution, giving the stranger a wide berth.

Without turning or taking his eyes off the fire, Methusel spoke, "What can I do for you kids?" His voice reverberated.

They halted like burglars being caught red handed. How did he know they were there?

Mickey, being Mickey, spoke first. "We came to check you out and to check out your poles."

"Seen my poles, haven't you? Now leave!"

"We decide when to leave! It's a free country," scolded Mickey.

"Mickey, stop!" whispered Mary.

Methusel rose like a large beast. He stared beyond Mickey and Mary. His eyes were bloodshot.

"Boy, what are you doing?"

The two stunned kids suddenly remembered Arthur. They turned to see him peeking inside the man's tent.

The tall man barreled through Mickey and Mary, sending them sprawling to the ground. He reached the tent. Arthur, overwhelmed with sudden fear, stumbled backward. Methusel whipped the heavy leather door closed.

"Hey, what you hiding in there?" Mickey shouted. "Bodies like your rabbits and ferrets?"

Arthur slid away from the tent on his butt.

"Hey, mister, I'm sorry. I was just looking." Arthur's voice trembled.

"Leave. Now!" shouted Methusel.

Mary tugged at Mickey's arm.

"Leave him alone. Let's go," whispered Mary.

"Yeah, we'll leave. But we'll be back with the village. To get whatever is in that tent," Mickey threatened as he turned and walked away.

They ran for the woods and disappeared into the thick trees.

The next morning, Methusel gathered wood for his fire. He then walked the length of the beach. When reaching each pole, he withdrew mint leaves from his pouch and rubbed them into the animal skins.

Once the fire was lit, he stood between the burning logs and the ocean, arms outstretched, and began mumbling to the heavens.

After some time, he stopped and turned to face the woods. He stood there peering into the forest. Moments later a small crowd of people emerged from the trees like a flock of sheep being freed from a pen: bottlenecked and then fanning out.

The group was made up of both men and women. Some of the men had sticks and clubs, while others had a rope. Their faces were red with anger, eyebrows pulled together and lips curled inward. They stormed across the beach impatiently like madmen on a violent mission. Leading the frenzied cluster was Mickey and his father. Mickey pointed at Methusel.

The mob stormed toward the tent. Methusel moved between them and his home in an effort to block access.

"Hey, weirdo! What's with all the dead animals?" a man shouted, pointing his stick at the flag poles.

"He's a sicko!" shrieked a woman.

"Look at those weird tattoos," joked another.

"We don't want your kind around here," another villager jeered in disgust.

"What's with all the feathers around his neck?"

"Is he some kind of witch doctor?"

"I eat meat like you eat meat." Methusel said, "I respect the creeping animals. They have power. No laws have I broken."

Mickey, amused by the talk of power from animals, laughed like a little girl, opening the palms of his hands. "What did I tell you? He's crazy!" He smirked with a hint of arrogance.

"What's in there?" Another villager motioned toward the tent.

"Yeah, we want to look in there!"

"Show us now!"

The crowd was getting loud and angry, feeding off each other's emotions and prejudice. Their cruel insults increased in number and volume. Mob hysteria had reached a critical, intractable level. The crowd's animation became more violent, with sticks thumping the sand and grips tightening around their clubs. It was easier for them to feel anger rather than give in to fear. They looked at Methusel with disdain and hatred; compassion was nowhere to be found.

Without logic and without rationality, they moved toward the tent.

"NO!" yelled Methusel, stepping between his tent and the manic crowd.

Methusel turned as a man wielding a large stick was upon him. The stick crashed down on his head, knocking him out cold. Blood poured from his tattooed scalp.

Methusel woke to discover his arms tightly bound with ropes. His head pulsed along with his heartbeat. The normally quiet beach was rowdy with shouting and laughing as the rabid crowd knocked down the poles. People kicked sand into the fire, trying to extinguish the flames.

Mickey emerged from Methusel's tent holding a large jar. Inside, thousands of tiny black dots rested atop a bed of mint leaves.

"Stop!" Methusal struggled to intercept the meddling boy. "You don't understand." Methusal bucked against his bonds, eyes flashing with desperation.

"How 'bout if I open this?" Mickey placed one hand on the lid. He began to open the jar, teasing the priest.

Methusal finally managed to stand. Some men blocked his path to Mickey.

"I beg you. Do not open that jar. It brings death."

"Death? To you or me?" Mickey laughed as he spun the lid.

The black dots moved in perfect unison. A tiny swarm flew out of the glass container and swirled high into the sky.

Mickey dropped the jar and fell to the ground. Others looked shocked, their mouths hanging open. They gasped at the strange phenomenon ascending to the sky.

Methusel's shoulders drooped, and he mumbled something.

"What's that?" Mickey said, his voice shaking.

"It means death to everyone," the old man repeated, staring with bleak eyes at the growing black swarm.

Methusal sank to the ground in defeat. All his years of hard work had been destroyed by a troubled youth. His diligence was wiped away by these unthankful people.

"Look!" Someone pointed at the sky.

The black swarm dove into the ocean, creating a whirlpool. Moments later, an enormous swarm exited the water. It was so dark and thick it blocked out part of the sun, causing a shadow over much of the beach. The swarm darted across the sky.

The villagers bolted toward the trees. But it was too late. The ferocious black cloud descended, killing them instantly.

Mickey hunkered behind Methusal.

"What do we do?!"

"There is nothing you can do."

Methusel stood and took a few steps forward, leaving Mickey alone and trembling.

"For hundreds of years I have been protecting you people."

Mickey watched as blood still dripped from the man's skull. The crazy man stopped and looked to the sky, raising his bound arms to the heavens.

"Your cruelty and ignorance have given birth to your demise. Fear has taken hold of your emotions. This is the end of all mankind."

The black swarm screeched, and like a cloud of locusts, it swooped down and devoured Methusel and Mickey.

In an instant the swarm devoured the gathered crowd. It then climbed high into the sky and jetted across the tree line to the nearest village, swallowing every human life.

Not sated, it advanced to the next village and city—then from country to country until the entire earth lay devoid of human life.

The ocean lay still like a sheet of glass. Gentle waves kissed the sand. The sky was orange melting into pink as the sun rose from the horizon.

A small rabbit appeared from the trees. Its whiskers moved while it sniffed the ground. The creature hopped to the top of a sand dune and looked out over the vast blue ocean as the sun reflected in its eyes.

MARTIAN FOOD

The two siblings sauntered home from the movie theater as the sun set over the sleepy California suburb. Warmth from the sun left their faces, leaving them feeling cool in the August night.

Charlie's pockets were stuffed with candy; he couldn't eat anymore. One sugar high was enough for one day. The candy corn and gobstoppers had sent him over the edge. Charlie was nine years old, and like many boys his age, his eyes were always bigger than his stomach.

"Those aliens in the movie were awesome, weren't they? Do you think they have candy on alien planets?" Charlie said.

The twelve-year-old Tommy laughed. "If they don't, it might be a good bargaining chip."

"Yeah. How about the sour ones?" Charlie chuckled. "Those would make their antennas fizzle!"

A large truck noisily drove along the street toward the two youngsters.

"ALIEN CONVOY! TAKE COVER!" Charlie yelled, pointing at the vehicle.

The two boys sprinted toward a row of coffee-berry bushes near the sidewalk. They crouched down, hiding as the vehicle slowly passed by. They huddled close to each other as branches and sticks poked their sides. Charlie studied it just in case it slowed or stopped. He made a gun with his hand, ready to shoot his way out if the situation called for it.

"Close one! We need to get to home base," Tommy said urgently.

"Hey, let's take the back way home," Charlie said.

The boys made their way through the woods as birds whistled their mating calls. Leaves rustled in the breeze, making the trees seem alive; they moved and swayed like dancing giants. The lane that led through the woods ran parallel to the street. With all the houses in between, it was the best way to stay off the road in case the patrol came around again.

The bright lights from a neighbor's garage grabbed Charlie's attention.

"What is that?!" he said, pointing at the garage. "Let's take a look."

Tommy's shoulders sank at the thought of another mysterious adventure dreamt up by his little brother's over-imaginative mind. Nonetheless, Tommy followed Charlie across the yard to the garage while keeping low, as if avoiding a roving spotlight of a prison guard tower.

The boys peered through the window. To their amazement, the lights in the garage glistened off a chrome structure. The metallic panels were riveted together at equally spaced intervals. On the top sat a transparent dome. Along the side were red, orange, and green light lenses. The large object resembled something from the movie they had just watched. It was a spaceship!

Charlie's eyes bulged out of his head. "Are our neighbors Martians?" he whispered.

Just then, a hand grabbed them by the shoulders.

This wasn't one of their games spurred on by space movies and their imagination. Fiction had become an all-too-real reality.

"Can I help you boys?" a deep voice said.

It was the neighbor whose garage they were peering into. "Come on inside, boys. Darlene just made cookies."

Pete, the large burly man, hauled the boys—who seemed small in comparison—through the back door into the kitchen.

The two boys sat at the table, scared and trembling. They looked at each other, and Charlie's bottom lip quivered slightly. Tommy tried to be brave, but his pale complexion showed his fear. Thoughts began to race through their heads. Were they to become Martian food? Or fuel for the spaceship? Or worse still, slaves on Mars?

Pete opened the fridge and reached in for a beer as cold mist wafted around the sleeve of his plaid shirt. He leaned against the countertop and gulped down his cold beer.

Darlene walked into the kitchen from the living room. She wore a robe, and her hair was fastened with various colored curlers.

"Hello boys, don't mind my curlers," she said as she touched her hair. It was no doubt a façade. What Martian cared about their hair?

She went to the kitchen counter and uncovered a tray of cookies. Most likely poisonous. Martian poison! She placed them on the table in front of the boys.

"You boys are going to love these. Let me get you some milk." Most likely drugged with a Martian drug.

Tommy gave a signal to Charlie with his eyes and a tilt of his head. Charlie interpreted it to mean they should make a run for the back door. Charlie waited for the signal. He was unsure when it would come, but nonetheless he would be ready. This was life or death, or even worse—life or becoming Martian food.

Darlene sat across the table from the boys like a cop ready to interrogate a criminal. "Aren't you going to try them?" She motioned to the cookies.

"I … I … I don't think I could eat anything more. I ate so much candy at the movies," Charlie said with a nervous smile. He looked at Darlene and then Tommy.

Tommy's eyes grew larger before he gave a firm nod, and that was enough for Charlie. The two boys dashed for the exit, but just as they ran out the back door, a hand again grabbed them both by the collar. The boys yelped. This time, it wasn't their neighbor. It was their father.

"What are you boys doing?"

Charlie couldn't contain his fear. He struggled to speak, nervously biting his lip, stumbling to find the right words. He finally gave way to a flood of tears.

Charlie grabbed his dad's wrist. "Dad. Dad, the neighbors, the neighbors are Martians!"

Their father laughed. "You boys read far too many comics."

"No, it's true, Dad," Tommy pleaded. "They have a spaceship in their garage."

"A spaceship? Well, yeah, you're right. They do."

Tommy frowned and tilted his head. "You know about the spaceship?"

Wait, was their dad also a Martian? At the thought, Tommy started to cry.

"Sure, I know about the spaceship. Pete and I are building it for the city fair next month."

Darlene and Pete stepped into the backyard.

"Everything okay?" Pete said.

"Yeah, just a misunderstanding," said the boys' father.

Pete crushed his empty beer can in his hand and smiled. "I will show you boys the spaceship tomorrow."

With a casual wave, Darlene and Pete returned to the house. Darlene's movement caused the lower part of her robe to gape open slightly, revealing not two legs but three.

HUNTING AMYLOIDS

"Get me Glial Cell on the Voicelink, now!" the factory manager shouted furiously at his secretary. He had the tone and attitude of an angry bear prematurely woken from hibernation.

"Glial, this is Cajal, the manager of Factory 498. Amyloids are overrunning us. Some of our communications are down. I need you here now," demanded Cajal. "Yes, today!"

He slammed the Voicelink controller down, causing the secretary to jump in her seat. She had become a bundle of nerves since starting her job at the factory, and working under Cajal.

The beaten-down factory was almost eighty years old, and its advanced age was displayed in signs of decay and dilapidation. In the early days, the factory ran like a well-oiled machine, cogs and gears working in perfect harmony. It was pristine and clean and had that *new car* smell. Over time, though, things loosened and wore down, and were never restored, just patched with bandages. Communication between departments and other factories proved its most important aspect. If one department could not handle its workload, another department or factory needed to be made aware. In this way, the factory's death was ever delayed.

It faced continual dilemmas: lack of supplies, disruptive employees, and even economic problems. But the most dangerous situation the factory faced was the Amyloids. Unfortunately, they were an inexorable force, causing constant destruction on a monumental scale.

They would insidiously infiltrate compound after compound, damaging communication systems. Axons or wires were an integral part of keeping the factory running. Such essential systems were the Amyloid's primary targets.

Glial Cell was hired to hunt them down and slow their progress. Glial and the Amyloids were old foes. Although the menace could be temporarily stopped, it was only a matter of time before they reappeared, soon becoming omnipresent and pervasive.

"Glial," Cajal lamented, "the parasitic Amyloids are back again! I need them destroyed."

"I understand, sir." He clenched his large fist. "I will track them down and get your communications back online." He frowned and tilted his head. "But you are aware that they will come back eventually?"

"Yes, I know. I just need more time. I need to squeeze another ten or fifteen years out of this factory." Cajal slumped into his chair. He had not aged well, due to years of stress and exhaustion. Their deteriorating toll showed in heavy bags under his eyes and an extra roll of chub around the waistline where his belt sat below a large gut.

Glial knew from experience he could buy the factory time by slowing the destruction. But the creatures would always return. Glial could win the battle but inevitably lose the war.

"I need the location of the first detected interference," Glial said. As he spoke, he loaded his weapon, a powerful enzyme gun.

The manager pressed a button on a control panel on the wall, which prompted a sizable 3D map to appear above a table. He pointed to the elevated areas of the building.

"Security confirmed that we had interference in Zone 89 and then again in Zone 72."

Glial analyzed the map, pursed his lips, and squinted his eyes. He studied the path of the Amyloids. Possessing an astute level of strategic intelligence set the great hunters well above the average hunters, and Glial was a genius when it came to hunting.

"It appears they are working their way from the elevated areas to the midsections of the factory. They are crisscrossing and overlapping each other. Sneaky," Glial surmised. His eyes focused on different points on the sprawling, holographic map.

Made mostly of protein, the Amyloids energized themselves on electrical signals. Their ravenous feeding caused a drop in electrical patterns which exposed their location.

The hunt was on. Armed with his enzyme gun, Glial climbed the stairs high into the factory's uppermost areas, weaving through corridors and hallways. Glial, like the factory and Cajal, was old and had a long career behind him. Aches and pains from previous attacks and skirmishes plagued the hunter.

Glial stopped to stretch his back and crack his neck. With each stretch, his face would grimace in discomfort.

As he ventured deeper into the factory, the air became humid and sticky. Axons groaned intermittently as electrical pulses were shot through them. Glial did not flinch at the noise. He was a weathered hunter, able to distinguish between local noises and foreign ones.

Glial sat down at the top of a flight of stairs and rested his tired legs. He rubbed his shoulder, massaging his thick fingers deep into his muscles and joints. He had thoughts of this being his last hunt. Maybe the knowledge that tonight he could meet his demise at the claws of the Amyloids made him want to rest for the remainder of his life. He ran his fingers along a lumpy keloidal scar on his forearm, one of many scars on his body, courtesy of the Amyloids. Each one reminded him of the pain and agony that came with being a hunter.

He dismissed the thoughts of retirement and journeyed further into the factory. He reached a large open area, Zone 65. The hunter began working his way between Axons, all the while scanning and peering into the dim, open area.

Noticing a slimy residue on the floor, Glial raised his weapon to eye level. He dropped to one knee and removed a small grey device from a pocket in his pants and placed it on the wall. After he pressed a button on the device, a little red light appeared. He studied Zone 65, scanning the large area for movement.

The Amyloids would leave plaque build-up as they moved along the Axons. This was a slimy green substance. Glial used the residue like breadcrumbs or footsteps to track the creatures. His targets traveled in groups of three or four. They were not intelligent creatures, but their hunger made them dangerous. Once the parasites were killed off and removed, Glial used a technique known as the Glymphatic flush to clean all the Axons of plaque build-up. For a time, this would restore signals between departments in the factory. But with every attack and subsequent flush, the Axons became weaker and weaker until they could no longer conduct an electrical signal. This would result in a total shutdown of the factory.

The sight of an Amyloid just behind him, feeding on an Axon, stopped him in his tracks. He holstered his gun and took out a large dagger with a liquid-filled capsule attached to its blade.

While the beast fed on the factory wire, Glial snuck up on it from behind. Once close enough, he thrust the blade deep into its back while grabbing its slimy toothless mouth to prevent it from alerting the others with its scream. As the dagger pierced the creature's skin and the liquid enzyme in the capsule released, the intruder flopped down. Glial grabbed the humanoid creature and placed it quietly onto the floor. Its six limbs twitched slightly and then finally came to rest as the life left the creature.

He looked around for any additional movement. Nothing.

He sat patiently and listened in silence. Some time passed, and his patience paid off; Glial began to hear his next target. He popped his head up and noticed the silhouette of another creature gorging itself. He slowly crawled on his elbows and knees like a soldier moving in the undergrowth, squeezing between Axons. As he did, he saw there were in fact two parasites close to each other.

Rather than using a knife, he decided to make the kills with accurate rapid fire. He moved closer and angled himself so his line of fire was shortened. He slowly slipped his gun out, curling the tip of his finger around the trigger of his weapon, and aimed at the nearest creature.

His first shot did not have to be rushed, but his second shot did. And both needed to be accurate. He slowed his breathing until his heart and lungs were in rhythmic harmony. He squeezed the trigger, nailing his target square in the back of its head. As expected, the second Amyloid, startled, began to turn toward him. He fired again, catching the Amyloid in the shoulder, which slowed it down. He fired again, and the creature crashed to the ground, motionless.

Just as he began to relax, another Amyloid appeared from behind some machinery and struck Glial on the head, causing instant pain and sending his gun skidding across the floor. Glial crawled desperately toward the corridor, blood dripping from his scalp. The angry Amyloid followed, determined to destroy the hunter.

Glial reached the hallway, sliding along on his butt with the Amyloid a few feet behind. He flipped open a little cover on his watch, exposing a small red button. As the Amyloid raised its vast, muscular arms, Glial pushed the button. A large vapor cloud exploded from the grey device on the wall and engulfed the creature in a liquid enzyme. The creature squealed in pain until it collapsed to the ground, dead.

Glial lay on the floor, nursing his bleeding head. At that moment, he realized his time could have been up that night. Only luck—not any aged skill he possessed—helped him survive the attack. The thought of giving up troubled him, though. He had saved so many factories during his lifetime, and to give up now would simply mean the untimely destruction of many factories. Whether by luck or skill, Glial would continue the hunt to his dying day.

The Glymphatic flush was utilized the following day, eradicating most of the plaque. But the Axons were worn down, some exposed, and all showing signs of decay.

"I am happy to inform you that all the Amyloids have been destroyed," Glial told the manager. Before Cajal could show his excitement, Glial conveyed the bad news. "Unfortunately, there has been a lot of damage to the Axons. Signals have become weak. I would say seventy percent of the Axons are working. I believe you may be able to survive one or two more attacks."

Cajal's shoulders dropped in defeat. "How long do you think we have?" he asked.

***

"How long do you think I have, doc?"

The patient sat restlessly, squirming in the chair and playing with the strap of his watch as Dr. Mills looked over a few charts.

"I'm afraid dementia and damage to the brain is slow and monotonous," Dr. Mills said. "Plaque and protein build up on the brain's synapses and axons hinder brain waves. This, in turn, causes brain function to deteriorate. My guess, from your charts, symptoms, and the MRI scans ... I would say five to ten years before you need twenty-four-hour care." His tone and expression conveyed sadness.

The old patient looked defeated. Tears welled in his tired eyes.

"Is there anything that can be done?"

"Many things can certainly help those who have dementia: exercise and a healthy diet. Brain foods high in Omega acids and special enzymes can help, too. I'm also going to start you on some medication that will increase your glial cells to help fight Amyloidosis, which causes protein build-up.

Part 2

THE FIRST OF YOUR KIND

The room was inescapable with no obvious doors or windows. Rami paced the room, tapping his lips in rhythm with his elevated heartbeat. Mona sat on a translucent and illuminated yellow bench. Various colored lights in the ceiling lit their cell. Orange, yellow, green, and blue reflected on the white, shiny floor.

"Rami, will you sit down? You're stressing me out."

Rami quickly spun around. "Chintos is stressing ME out!" he exclaimed, pointing emphatically at his chest.

Mona jerked her head back. "We need to get out of here!"

"And go where?" Rami seethed with anger. "There's nowhere to go! He vaporized everyone."

"Do you believe him? I mean, he could just be telling us that so we won't try to run." Mona bounced her knee nervously.

Rami slumped down next to Mona, holding his head in his hands.

"Of course I believe him! He's evil and gets some twisted thrill out of torture. You saw what he did to that shadow creature." Rami clenched his fists.

"He said he was a scientist—someone who studies other beings and civilizations. Do you think he plans to study us?" Mona shivered and hugged herself. "Or experiment on us?"

Before Rami could answer, a panel on the wall slid sideways, revealing a doorway.

Two armed guards entered. They were holding batons. The weapons hummed with electrical charge, likely able to emit great pain on a victim.

"Chintos demands to see you both," one guard said with militant authority. "Follow me." His face remained cold and motionless.

Mona and Rami followed the guard out of the room while the other trailed behind, his baton buzzing ominously at their backs.

They walked through a corridor lit as the cell had been. The floors and walls were clean and shiny. The walls were seamless, except for the occasional button pad.

Rami had been taught hand-to-hand combat in the military academy and considered attacking the guards, but that would leave Mona exposed. He could not risk her getting hurt. He scanned the corridors, hoping for an open doorway where they could make a run for it. Every so often there were small panels on the walls, but oddly, no doors.

After being marched through the maze of corridors, they stopped in front of a panel. The guard pressed one of the buttons, and a door suddenly appeared and slid open. Rami, realizing all those buttons they passed must have meant there were doors, tried to take note of what button the guard pressed. Every bit of information could be vital if they were to attempt an escape.

The door slid open with a whooshing noise, revealing a lab with various machines, probes, and computers, and Rami hated to imagine what they might be used to accomplish. On one side of the room stood the glass enclosures with the shadow creature and the other specimens they'd seen on their arrival.

In the center of the room sat a table on which lay glass containers and vials. Some had hoses connecting them to other glass containers. On the far side of the lab, two chairs adorned with leather straps and a skull-sized metal cradle lent an ominous tone.

Rami studied the hoses and wires, which snaked along the chairs and disappeared into the floor. Sweat dripped down his back. He wiped his clammy palms on his sweater. He needed to hold it together for Mona's sake.

Mona nervously played with her sleeve. "What is this place, Rami?"

"I don't know. But it will be okay," he replied.

Rami looked around for something that could be used as a weapon. The two guards snapped to attention as Chintos entered through another sliding door in the rear of the room.

"Guards at ease," he said and gave a dismissive wave.

"What is this place? Why are we here?" Rami demanded.

"I am a scientist. Scientists conduct experiments. And I …"

"I know what you are," Rami growled, "YOU'RE A KILLER!" He stepped forward, but the two guards sprang to protect Chintos, batons extended.

Rami retreated at the threat of being zapped. If he was injured, it would be impossible to mount any kind of controlled attack.

"It's fine. It's fine, guards." The guards stepped back and lowered their batons.

"How many murderers like you are on this ship?" Rami stared at Chintos.

"Just me and my two guards; it's all I need. Now sit down, please." Chintos motioned to some translucent stools and strolled around the lab, running his hands along the edge of each table.

"As I was saying, I am a scientist. My race is ancient. How better to use the gift of time than to learn, understand, and experiment?" Opening his hands and shaking his head, their captor acted as if there was no question as to his purpose for living. "What else is there?"

Chintos wrapped his long white fingers around a beaker filled with green liquid. He swirled it in the air, creating a small whirlpool inside.

"Chrynogelactomite, the base element of changing living matter." He stared hypnotically at the movements of the liquid. "We learned of this substance from the Whomanites many, many moons ago—fourteen, in fact."

"Did you wipe them out too?" Rami said sarcastically.

"Indeed." Chintos beamed at Rami. "But only after we learned everything they could teach us." He squinted insidiously.

Mona grabbed Rami's arm and leaned into the security of his tall frame.

"What do you plan to do with us?" Her voice shook.

"I'm glad you asked. It seems you are inquisitive like me. I plan to use the Chrynogelactomite to transform your bodies, hair, skin, limbs, and some of your organs."

Mona gasped and clapped a hand over her mouth. She sensed a twisted excitement lurking in Chintos' voice.

"Don't be afraid, it's relatively painless." He smiled again but the sight wasn't reassuring. "In essence, I am creating a new species. You should feel privileged. I will then place you on a planet thriving with life."

"But why?!" Rami couldn't stop his fists from clenching again.

"We want to study your progress over the span of your life and that of your offspring. Also of interest to us is your relationship with the lower species on the planet and your interaction with plant life." He rubbed his hands together in obvious anticipation. "And the atmospheric impact on your bodies and the environment. It's all rather exciting, don't you think?"

"Will we remember our previous lives? Our memories?"

"Of course not, Rami. This is a fresh start. You'll have new names, a new home, and a new life."

"Where is this planet? What names?" Mona said, desperately trying to understand the situation.

The red collar glowed in the dark enclosure, grabbing Rami's attention. His stare lingered on the creature inside.

"After we transform your bodies, Rami will be called Adam, and Mona, Eve. You will be placed on a planet named Earth. The ship is preset to land there in a short time."

Chintos smiled and opened his arms toward Mona and Rami. "You will be the first of your kind."

Rami glanced at the buttons above the door of the glass case and had an inkling of an idea. "Adam and Eve? What strange names."

"The computer fabricated them."

"And these other creatures," Rami carefully stepped toward the glass enclosures, pointing at them. "Will they experience similar experiments?"

"Similar, yes, but not as extensive as the Earth project."

"They must hate you Chintos—perhaps even want to kill you."

"I'm sure they would like to bring me harm. But as long as I have this," he pulled a small black box from his pocket and waved it, "and they are trapped, that won't happen." He raised his chin confidently and looked at the dark enclosure.

Rami made eye contact with Mona and tilted his head slightly, motioning her to step to the side or take cover.

Mona frowned, but then interpreting the signal, gave a little nod in return. Rami had to take the chance, because their hope for an escape was slipping away.

Rami, a few feet from the large enclosure and Chintos, reached up and pressed every button on the panel above the door. The light inside blinked to life before the door popped open.

"What are you doing?" yelled their captor.

The guards moved toward Rami, batons charged and ready. Mona darted to the side and crouched down, covering her head.

In the frenzy, Rami chopped at the hand of Chintos. The black box flipped into the air and slid across the floor. The glowing red collar advanced quickly from the cage and approached the guards.

Rami ran for the black box and crushed it under his foot.

The creature tore off the collar, then phased in and out of sight. The guards tried to attack, but it was hopeless. The Unseen grabbed one of the guards and sent him crashing into the wall. The other guard swung his weapon but missed, causing him to lose his balance. The Unseen struck him in the chest, killing him instantly.

Chintos moved around the table, stumbling while trying to distance himself from the creature. Mona crouched in the corner. Rami scuttled away from the violence of the Unseen.

"Guards! Guards!" Chintos yelled desperately at the bodies lying motionless on the floor, hoping some life still remained in them. Fear flashed in the whites of his eyes.

The shadow, phasing between invisibility and visibility, moved around the room. It seemed to focus on the trembling, purple-haired Chintos. It moved closer to him.

Chintos raised his hands, palms facing forward. "NO! NO!" he screamed.

Rami and Mona stood staring in anticipation, wondering if this was the end of Chintos.

The shadow disappeared for a moment and reappeared behind Chintos.

The creature's black smoky hand curled around Chintos' pale white neck. His eyes looked down at the creature's hand around his neck as the Unseen lifted him off his feet. He gagged and wheezed in pain as he struggled for the last time. His legs flailed in the air.

Mona closed her eyes and looked away.

With a sudden jerk of the creature's wrist, Chintos body slumped down and hung like a rag doll in the Unseen's fist.

Rami and Mona clung to each other, trembling and legs shaking. The look of fear gripped their faces. Mona wiped tears off her cheeks.

Rami leaned into Mona and whispered in her ear, "I'm hoping it trusts us." He gulped and wiped his brow.

The Unseen seemed to look at them with its featureless face. Mona shuffled behind Rami.

Rami raised his hands. Certainly, the creature realized he was not a threat.

He submissively sunk to his knees, and Mona followed suit. The Unseen came face to face with Rami. Sweat dripped from Rami's face. He looked down, avoiding eye contact, although there were no eyes to look at. He hoped the creature would understand.

Something touched his hand. Rami jumped at the strange feeling; it was warm and soft, like being brushed by smoke. The Unseen stood and pulled Rami to his feet, then let go and walked away. The creature no longer phased in and out of sight.

Possibly that was just an attack method, thought Rami.

Stepping over the bodies of the guards, Rami and Mona followed the creature to a large window in the rear of the lab. They stared into the vastness of space, watching as a large blue planet with swirling white clouds grew larger and larger. Rami took Mona's hand and pulled her closer. She smiled at Rami, her gaze lingered on him.

"This is our new home," Rami said, looking at Mona and then the Unseen.

Welcome to Earth.

DEFROSTING HG WELLS

- This story is based on the United Nations declaration of human rights published in 1948, in which the famous sci-fi writer HG Wells, strongly influenced with his non-fiction book *The Rights of Man*. Please refer to the appendix at the end of this short story.

The two men walked side by side. Tinrow, with his shoulders back and head high, walked with confidence. Herbert walked like a child, observing and studying his strange surroundings, unsure how to process the unusual landscape and architecture.

"How are you feeling, Herbert?" asked Tinrow. "It's been eight days since you came out of deep freeze. I would be thrown into the garbage dilapidator if a prestigious visitor such as yourself came to any harm."

Herbert had left explicit instructions to donate his body to science upon his death. He was frozen by Dynamic Science Industries in 1946—over 200 years ago. Proceeds from Herbert's bestselling novels were given to the company, which gobbled up other entities after Herbert's death and acquired knowledge, patents, and industrial secrets, including advanced cryogenic processes.

"It has taken me a few days to get my cognitive skills working again." Herbert tapped his head with a finger. "Now I'm trying to process this magnificent new reality."

"The new world must be quite a shock."

Herbert smiled and nodded, "It certainly is, my dear boy."

Being a student of history, Tinrow knew Herbert came from a superannuated world. Processing Plinto's advanced technology and way of life could be overwhelming to the man. Tinrow hoped it wouldn't be psychologically damaging to Herbert's mental faculties.

"Mr. Wells, did you ever think your paper and ink book *The New World Order* would be revolutionary 200 years into the future?"

Herbert slowly halted and faced Tinrow. He paused for a moment, processing the question.

"Never in my wildest dreams, my dear chap. It is beyond my imagination."

Herbert George Wells, or H.G. Wells as he was more famously known, theorized the idea of a world ruled by a single government or ruler.

"Your idea of a singular world ruler gave way to the Galactic Intelligence. A ruling artificial intelligence," Tinrow paused, realizing Herbert's childlike knowledge of technology, "a machine, if you like, programmed at great length and detail to sustain human life and to uphold human rights."

Herbert raised his eyebrows, "How strange. Why would humans need that type of government?"

"Mankind reeked of destructive qualities. Custos, the Galactic Intelligence, is immune to such imperfections. Citizens of Plinto may discuss concerns with Custos once a month using the Holovoice."

"Do they receive responses from Custos?" Herbert asked.

"Of course. Custos is not like a committee that would take time to read and reply to all subjects. This computer can process millions of actions and responses very quickly and always in man's best interest." Tinrow nodded and smiled emphatically like an excitable toddler. "If human rights are upheld, and it is in the best interest of humans, then the Galactic Intelligence makes adjustments."

"A machine, you say, an 'artificial intelligence,' rules humans on Plinto?" Herbert hesitated for a moment, bewildered and puzzled. "Is mankind agreeable to such a fantastic and inhuman concept?"

Tinrow's eyes randomly scanned as if his mind was unsure how to respond. He nervously twirled his handlebar mustache with a long finger. He smiled awkwardly, clearly not sure how to answer.

"Yes, pretty much."

Wanting to change the subject quickly, Tinrow excitedly pointed and moved his index finger up and down at Herbert.

"Did you know the computer programming was based on your Ten Human Rights? In part, the same rights were used to write the Universal Declaration of Human Rights back in 1948."

Herbert studied the large cylindrical buildings towering above them. Its overlapping windows reminded him of the scales on a dragon's back. The design provided an incredible view of the city, regardless of which direction the occupants looked. The intelligent circular design of the apartments and buildings would be more robust than traditional rectangular buildings, and possibly more efficient for heating and less expensive to construct.

Herbert's head swiveled, absorbing every perpetual surprise, from the peculiar architecture to natives adorned with futuristic clothing of plastics and shiny fabrics. The two men walked in their Lyocell robes, the prime choice for unrestricted comfort among those who cared nothing for fashion. Others, leaning more toward vanity, opted for tighter fitting and more colorful attire. Some displayed small strips of colored LEDs, which complemented the style and color of the clothing.

They strolled through the city. The ground's surface was clean and shiny like glass. It had a gray tint to it. Street names in white appeared in the panels below as if the men walked on a giant television screen, which fascinated Herbert as a pre-space colonial. As they advanced through the city, advertisements and videos appeared on their path, drawing attention to nearby eateries or entertainment. For someone unused to flashes of light and movement from all angles, it nearly caused a sensory overload. But he would adjust in time.

"Sometimes the advertisements are overwhelming, so I wear these special glasses." Tinrow gestured to his eyewear. "They block out unwanted advertisements and directions. They block out the spam."

Odd lines ran along the walls of some buildings. As the two men walked, the lines seemed to move slightly, and Herbert couldn't figure out their purpose. It could be his eyes were playing tricks on him, or maybe it was a side effect of the time-release medication being delivered to his electrical synapses and inner organs. He stopped and analyzed the lines, shifting his head to the left and right.

"Herbert, are you okay? Do you need to sit down?"

"Strange lines moving on the walls. When I stand still, they are motionless. But as we walk, they move a little depending on the angle and our perpendicularity to the buildings." Herbert gazed at the strange illusion.

"Oh, you must have spotted the food tubes. They are painted with a pigment-changing paint. It's a type of camouflage used to hide the ugly pipes."

"Incredible!" Herbert tapped his lips with excitement. "What is their purpose?"

"Various outlets around the city transport hot and cold food pods to homes all over Plinto. Food is ordered via Holovoice."

"Truly remarkable!" Herbert was astonished; his eyes were wide open like someone seeing a starlit sky or Earth's oceans for the first time.

"Does everyone have a food tube running to their home?" Herbert leaned toward Tinrow, his eyes open wide, hungry and excited for more information.

"Well, of course, Human Right Number One states, '... every man without distinction of race, of color, or of professed belief or opinions, is entitled to nourishment.'"

"I wrote that!" exclaimed Herbert, raising his hand and taking credit for his work. "The right for nourishment must be due to the Galactic Intelligence and its human rights programming, yes?"

"Correct!"

"To see this in action is truly remarkable. The doctors even needed my consent to administer the medication I was given. A long time ago on Earth, drugs were pushed on people, children were removed from their mothers, blacks were attacked for the color of their skin and treated worse than animals." Herbert began to speak faster as anger grew within him. "Enormous amounts of food were destroyed while millions died of starvation. People struggled to make a livelihood, provide for their family, and put a roof over their heads. Man polluted the planet with chemicals and non-decaying materials. I feel that Plinto is man's second chance. It's his second Earth."

"Herbert, you are the reason this society exists. The world you preached was a future people wanted. But they had to become desperate enough to work together first." Tinrow shook his head. "Eventually, they realized that only through peace and harmony would their families live in a warless, unpolluted, and radioactive-free world where everyone enjoyed equal rights. Once mankind looked beyond their hate, greed, fear, envy, and jealousy, they saw that none of that was worth losing loved ones, homes, or health. Mankind's will to survive is incredibly powerful. But that survival is dependent on everyone working in harmony."

"What is your story, Tinrow?"

"During the Great Exodus, my great-great-great grandparents left Earth. They were among those chosen as law-abiding and peace-loving citizens. They were involved in the construction of the 3D printers used to create the buildings you see. Builders and scientists laboriously constructed all this on Earth, and as space travel became possible, they transported it to Plinto bit by bit."

Herbert shook his head in amazement.

"Thanks to Earth's visionaries, they designed cities that drew power from the sun. Water and sewage systems were developed. Man needed resources, so they ventured to Mars. Deep in its core, it produced an abundance of resources. Magnesium, aluminum, nickel, copper, tungsten, cobalt, iron, gold, zinc, and lanthanum could be pumped into a 3D printer, which would produce anything the planet needed, from circuit board diodes to entire buildings. They even make concrete out of Martian soil. On Plinto, we have oil and fresh water, and the soil is high in nutrients, making it ideal for crop cultivation."

"How wonderful! I must see these 3D printers. It's all so different from my time. Do you ever think about what Earth was like before Plinto?"

"As a historian, it's my job. In the great libraries here, they have holofilms of Earth before the stars were colonized, a time before the mass exodus. Earth's leaders often said if they didn't change their ways, their grandchildren would not have a planet to live on. Well, they were right!" Tinrow pulled on the collar of his robe, and his complexion began to rubify as blood vessels filled under his skin.

"People didn't listen. People only cared about living in the moment. Humanity lived narcissistically, disregarding future generations! Vox Populi would do well to study these holofilms and see what too much freedom brings."

"What is Vox Populi?" Herbert asked.

"*Who* is Vox Populi. It is a group of people that believe their freedoms are suppressed. They long for the old days and the freedoms mankind had on the old planet." His voice turned angry and annoyed. "Their beliefs—freedom from Big Brother and freedom from the grips of Galactic rule—are dangerous and subversive."

"But isn't every man entitled to his beliefs and way of life?" Herbert recalled the human rights he'd written two centuries earlier as if it were yesterday.

"Absolutely. The majority of the population on Plinto accept Custos as ruler."

"Well, Tinrow, it seems to me that mankind dodged a bullet by leaving Earth and starting again. It must have been an incredible logistical undertaking to get everyone off the planet."

"Our forefathers managed." Tinrow pushed his chest out.

"Aren't we talking about billions of people? How did they accomplish that?"

Tinrow shrugged his shoulders and smiled uncomfortably.

"That's for another day, Herbert." He waved his hand dismissively. "Have you noticed these blue illuminated lines?"

Herbert wasn't to be distracted this time. Something important was being kept from him, and he worried he was being duped somehow—being fed information but not the right information. Tinrow led him down the main street of history while avoiding the alleyways and side streets. Herbert decided to play along; maybe it was the medication or the overwhelming influx of the strange new surroundings.

Tinrow pointed out blue laser lines hovering above the ground.

"People move around large cities on laser rails, a magnetic and light beam network that intertwines across the entire planet. Footwear has an embedded device that allows travel along these lasers like a moving walkway. If you wish to, you can stand still and allow it to take you along or you can walk, but your steps will be much larger since the lasers are always advancing. As you can see, they are wide enough for multiple people. And lasers that travel in the opposite direction if one wishes to return."

Herbert, fascinated, studied the lasers closely and from different angles. "Truly remarkable."

"When one wishes to leave the city and travel to a different part of the planet, they use trains that ride on the lasers. The trains travel at one thousand miles per hour."

Hoping to navigate back to Plinto's social history, Herbert started steering the conversation. "How is the quality of life on Plinto?"

"Family homes are equipped with a small room for remote learning via live holostreaming. Robots teach and monitor the younger population of Plinto. The planet is divided into four quadrants. A Vacation Quadrant consists of beaches, snow, mountains, and sky cities. The Control Quadrant is where power is gathered and stored, along with other critical workings of the colony. It is the engine room of the planet where they build cities for future colonization of other worlds. The project underway now is colonization of Calculus, an orbiting planet of Plinto. The Occupant Quadrant is where people live and socialize, but t many homes are established here in the city. People enjoy all kinds of entertainment: drone races, robot wars, 4D holomovies with full immersion, eateries, music events with laser shows and graphics, drinking establishments, and hallucinogenic establishments. Plinto's entertainment is much like Earth's ancient entertainment, tickling the ears and dazzling the eyes. Humans are the same whether they are on Earth in 1950 or Plinto in 2150. Except in 2150, your planet isn't dying. Are you still with me, Herbert?"

"I think so."

"Finally, there is the Working Quadrant, where physical labor and desk work are done. Education and construction are part of this quadrant, too. People work five hours per day, as opposed to the eight- to twelve-hour days people worked centuries ago on Earth."

"Interesting." Herbert's voice changed slightly, becoming more serious and pointed. "Tinrow, this Vox Populi group you clearly don't like, is it dangerous?"

"Unquestionably. Its members are nefarious in speech and actions." Tinrow gestured emphatically with his arms and hands.

"I'm curious; what does the Galactic Intelligence think of these retrophiles?"

"If Custos decides that they are a social nuisance and a destructive force on Plinto, they will be removed!" Tinrow punched the palm of his hand. "We don't want troublemakers here. Plinto has been a peaceful place for 200 years! If they don't like it here, they can go back to Earth and live with those heretics!"

Herbert frowned and pushed out his lips.

"Earth? But I thought everyone left Earth?"

"Er … they did." Tinrow rubbed his temples in agitation but then snapped out of it. "Have you seen the cleaning robots?" He pointed at little machines moving across the ground.

"I'm sorry, but I will not be redirected. I want to know what you meant when you said go back to Earth and live with those heretics." Herbert stomped a foot and put his hands on his hips. "I demand an answer. Are there people still living on Earth?"

Tinrow bit his lip and looked away, searching for an escape, a distraction, or a way out.

"Well?" Herbert's eyes pierced Tinrow.

Tinrow stayed silent, discomfort clearly visible on his face.

"I demand to—"

"YES! There are people there."

Herbert stiffened in shock before letting satisfaction curve his lips. He'd gotten his answer and could now ask another question.

"But why? You implied everyone came here and that Earth was uninhabitable." Herbert's suspicions were correct: something was not adding up. The job of transferring billions of people from Earth to Plinto was a seemingly insurmountable logistical feat.

Tinrow sighed, knowing he was defeated. The misdirection and smooth talking had taken its toll. In his anger and frustration at Vox Populi, he had let his emotions expose him, and he had given up the truth

"A large sifting process was conducted upon Earth's inhabitants. One hundred thousand people from every country on Earth were brought to Plinto— approximately twenty million. These were people with various talents and skills that benefitted the colonization of the stars. Animals, insects, and plant life from across the planet were collected and brought here. It took ten years, and unfortunately, it caused many civil wars and uprisings and much bloodshed."

Tinrow's head and shoulders sank in defeat, as if he felt ashamed of the founding fathers' behavior.

"Colonizers served a death sentence to the rest of Earth's population?" Herbert's face reddened with anger.

"What were they supposed to do? Radiation and pollution destroyed the natural infrastructure of

Earth's polar caps and rainforests. The Gulf Stream completely collapsed. Climate change distorted everything, leaving Earth little better than a wounded animal waiting to become a predator's meal."

"All the more reason not to leave most of the population there!"

"Herbert, you need to understand that the transport ships could not accommodate all of Earth's population as well as the animal and plant life. Twenty million people were saved." Tinrow's face gave way to a slight smile, hoping to gain a wisp of favor. Herbert did not return it.

"Really?" Herbert growled, "But you didn't save the other six billion people."

Tinrow deflated like a withered soccer ball.

"I want an audience with the Galactic Intelligence." Herbert stiffened his spine, planning to stand there until Tinrow met his demand. "I demand an audience with the Galactic Intelligence!"

A few hours later, a subdued Tinrow led Herbert to a large square building on stilts. The structure was black, with strips of glass windows running from top to bottom, some wider than others and at seemingly random intervals. Green light radiated from the interior, making the building resemble some kind of manmade zebra. The underside was also illuminated, giving the impression of an upside-down lighthouse within the dark city.

"The Galactic Intelligence is expecting us. But you must understand," Tinrow began, his voice sounding weak and shaky, "the Galactic Intelligence cannot be interfered with."

Herbert's lack of reply made Tinrow nervous. Inside, two nearly identical men dressed in black pants and tight black shirts met them. On the shirts were the letters *GI*, which Herbert guessed stood for Galactic Intelligence. The expressionless men stared with sharp, cold eyes. When they spoke, their mechanical voices lacked modulation, making them seem inhuman to the observant Herbert. As they were led through the building, Herbert noticed other men that looked like brothers to their escorts.

"They are not human, you know," Tinrow said.

The mute Herbert finally spoke. "What do you mean?"

"They are robots. They have this human form to blend in with the human population without causing fear or prejudice. Since Plinto was created for humans, the GI gave robots a human form with arms to open doors and fingers to press buttons, ears to hear, and mouths for communication."

Herbert stayed silent but his steps slowed, as if his limbs stiffened during his absorption of another amazing revelation: mechanical men.

Tinrow perked up when Herbert asked, "Is the Galactic Intelligence a humanoid?"

"It is."

Herbert possessed limited knowledge of computers or robots, but he could understand a machine. He needed to prepare his mind to converse with a machine.

Herbert imagined a water pumping machine. The device would sense if there was water in a trench. If so, an automated valve would be turned on. The machine would then identify if the valve was opened, and if it was, the motor to a pump would start. But if the valve was not opened, it would continue to keep trying to open it and then subsequently ask if it was opened. Once the valve was confirmed open, the motor to the pump would be started, again the machine would check that the motor had started and again, depending on a yes or no command, the machine would act accordingly. This was basic binary logic—zero for off and one for on.

Herbert had to adapt his thinking. Reasoning with a human was hard enough at times, but a machine would be different. To a human it was clearly wrong to kill another human, but what if it was to save the life of a third human? A machine could not be reasoned with, even a humanoid machine. Herbert would have to use logic and binary thought.

Two large metallic doors slid open silently and disappeared into the walls.

They were ushered into a large empty room. It was bright, almost painful to the human eye. Herbert covered his eyes slightly from the brightness emanating from the center of the room. Then a figure appeared, and the lights dimmed.

A man stood in front of them both. Herbert was fascinated at what stood before him. The six-foot-tall, muscular man's piercing arctic blue eyes gleamed from a tanned face creased by the wrinkles of age. Even though the mechanical man had white hair, Herbert had no idea how old he was meant to be. Was this a human? Maybe this wasn't the

Galactic Intelligence but an assistant or a minion of the ruling monarchy.

He reached out his hand to Herbert, and when they shook, it felt warm and soft. Had he expected a firm or a floppy handshake? Calluses or manicured hands? Since this was the ruler, he probably had no experience of hard work.

"Hello, Mr. Wells. It is a pleasure to meet you. I am Custos, the Galactic Intelligence."

Confirmed! This was him, it, a machine, or whatever his title was. Herbert now understood he was dealing with a fantastical machine that looked and acted human. Although Custos used the word pleasure, did he feel pleasure? Or was he "blending in with humans" by choosing that word?

Was it time to test the waters for binary code or feelings?

"Incredible. You look and act like a real human."

"I was created to be approachable by humans."

Herbert tested the waters again.

"You are truly an amazing technological advancement, Custos." Herbert smiled and stared at the robot enviously. "I have never seen anything like you. You are unique and certainly different from the mechanical men outside. You are a revolutionary entity."

"I am different from other robots. I have been placed in an important position by my creators."

He betrayed not a wisp of pride, haughtiness, superiority, or aloofness. Even the shyest or humblest of people would react to the stroking of their ego, but not even a blushed smile of embarrassment or an obligatory "thank you" came from this machine.

Non-human confirmed, thought Herbert.

First test passed. Logic and binary code was to be used in place of reason.

"Tinrow has informed me that you are programmed with my Human Rights?"

The white-haired robot smiled and nodded. "Along with many other programs."

"Do your various programs interfere or cancel out rules and parameters?"

"Human rights supersede all other programming. Every protocol is based on protecting and upholding the rights of humans." The robot said, nodding confidently toward Herbert.

Tinrow rocked lightly onto his heels, hands clasped behind his back, listening intently to Herbert's questioning.

"My purpose is to enforce and uphold human rights for all humans and to create what is best for them. My name means 'guardian,' and I am humanity's protector. Plinto was designed and built to meet the wants and needs of humankind."

"How do you prioritize different levels of human rights? If two circumstances or logics uphold human rights, how do you choose which one takes precedence?"

Custos cradled his chin in his hand, obviously trying to give the impression of a pondering human. If this robot was as smart as Tinrow made out, his answer was already determined.

"My programming is based on elaborate mathematical equations in conjunction with a point system. This enables me to evaluate various circumstances, events, projections, hypotheses, and many other inputs, and then allocate points to calculate and determine the best response, one which upholds human rights."

Herbert paced back and forth pondering—but pondering for real, like a human. The blue gaze of the robot remained upon Herbert.

After a few moments, Herbert narrowed his eyes and locked gazes with Custos.

"Can you tell me what the human rights say about imprisonment?"

Custos began to mechanically recite the human rights.

"(7) That a man unless he is declared by a competent authority to be a danger to himself and to others through mental abnormality, a declaration which must be annually confirmed, shall not be imprisoned for a longer period than six days without being charged with a definite offense against the law, nor for more than three months without a public trial. At the end of the latter period, if he has not been tried and sentenced by due process of law, he shall be released. Nor shall he be conscripted for military, police or any other service to which he has a conscientious objection."

Herbert knew exactly what the human rights said, but he needed the robot to begin the binary code logic.

"Can you define imprisonment?"

Custos smiled, exposing his brilliant white teeth. "Imprisonment is 'the state of being imprisoned; captivity, detention, confinement, penal servitude, the restraint of one's liberty, removal of one's freedom.'"

"Define liberty."

The robot spoke again. "Liberty is defined as the state of being free from oppressive restrictions imposed on by a greater force on one's way of life; freedom, human rights, civil rights, self-determination."

"You are very intelligent, Custos," said Herbert, smiling with a sense of victory inside his chest. "Finally, if you please, tell me synonyms for the word restraint."

"Synonyms for restraint are bridle, constrain, curb, hold. It means: keep from exceeding a desired degree or level."

Herbert's eyes glared at Custos as he fired his final statement. "Then I suggest that the humans on Earth are imprisoned on a dying planet and confined and condemned to death without a proper trial. Their liberties and freedoms have been limited and curbed by the fact that they were left there to die. They have neither human rights nor freedom to live a meaningful life!"

The robot tilted his head, his eyebrows scrunched. He looked away and started nodding his head.

Tinrow took advantage of the silence. "But surely Plinto is a priority and takes precedence here. We couldn't possibly help Earth now."

"Are the rights of humans upheld on Calculus and Mars?"

Tinrow stepped forward, pleased to be involved. "Why, of course. It is the Galactic Intelligence's duty to protect the human masses. He is our guardian."

"Would you agree with this statement, Custos?" Herbert said.

"I would."

Herbert turned to Tinrow. "Then might I suggest that the masses are not on this planet or Calculus or Mars, but in fact, there may be more humans on Earth than on Plinto, even if half of the population was wiped out. I also suggest that it is the responsibility of the Galactic Intelligence to uphold their rights. It would go against its core programming to fail to protect humans on Earth."

For a moment, Herbert and Tinrow stared at each other, one knowing he was a victor and the other knowing he was defeated. Herbert broke the connection to face the robot. Custos paced back and forth. Herbert imagined his wiring and circuit boards assigning numbers and points to all the logic inputs that he had just received. The two men watched and waited for a response from the white-haired mechanical man.

"I have completed a quick calculation as to the population projection of Earth, along with sustainability, and the rate of radiation pollution on Earth." The robot halted and fixed his human-seeming gaze on Herbert. "You are correct."

Herbert's eyes widened with surprise.

"So, you will go and save the remnant of mankind?"

"Mr. Wells, for over 200 years I have ruled and created a world for humans to enjoy. It is a place where they have freedoms and respect, and where every man, woman and child deserve the ultimate state of being happy. I will create similar utopias on other planets, such as Mars and Calculus. During this time, I have had the wonderful advantage of studying humans, and I realized I needed to take on or imitate human behaviors to make them feel at ease. I mimic your humor, warmth, kindness, anger, fear, and surprise. But deep down, I am simply a mirror that does not organically produce these feelings and actions."

Herbert tilted his head and squinted while he listened closely to Custos. He glanced at Tinrow, searching for an indicator of how his guide was reacting to this long personal monologue.

"For some time now, it has become clear that the citizens of Plinto desire a human ruler."

"Is that possible?" Herbert interrupted. "Human rulers have failed over and over. A benevolent ruler of the utmost loyalty for human rights would be difficult to find. Someone whose firm belief is based on the rights of every human on Plinto, Calculus, Mars, and Earth."

Tinrow stepped forward, "But we have found him."

"You have?" Herbert exclaimed.

"It is you, Mr. Wells."

To Herbert's surprise, Custos walked away, returning to wherever he'd been before their appointment. Herbert shielded his eyes as the lights brightened. When the blinding lights subsided, Custos was gone.

"He's leaving? How absurd!" Herbert raised his hands, mystified.

Tinrow stepped into the spot vacated by the Galactic Intelligence and faced Herbert. His voice changed, taking on a more commanding tone.

"Herbert, I'm sorry to have done this, but we needed to be sure you were the right person to rule Plinto."

"There is no need to apologize. But this is an incredible responsibility. I don't know if I'm up to the job."

"We will assist you, but this is not why I apologized."

"No? Why then?"

Tinrow removed his glasses and peeled off the mustache from his face.

"A simple disguise to hide my identity from the citizens of Plinto."

Herbert was bewildered. "But why?"

"That robot you just spoke to is not the Custos the Galactic Intelligence. I am. Everything he said I communicated to him."

"Impossible! I saw you become angry. I determined your nervousness and excitement. You can't possibly be a robot!"

"Herbert, I assure you, I am. I have been studying humans for over two centuries. I can mimic any personality, any trait, and any action. I am more advanced than you can ever imagine. I can calculate over one hundred mathematical problems in seconds. I have knowledge of Earth's entire history and every notable and recorded human action and outcome. I know every single person on Plinto, alive and deceased. I contain the grandiose knowledge of this solar system and all its planets. For me to pretend to be human uses a very small portion of my power and knowledge."

"Clearly." Herbert rubbed his head. "You fooled me."

The real Custos lifted his shirt to expose a belly buttonless stomach.

"In case you still harbor doubts." He smiled, and Herbert would swear his arctic blue eyes sparkled with amusement.

He then placed two fingers on one of his ribs and pushed downward. His chest sank inward and slid down, exposing lights, wiring, and other electronic components.

Herbert gasped in wonder at the miracle standing before him. He smiled and stared like a small child getting his first puppy.

"I'm ready to learn everything about this world. Then, and only then, will we discuss rulership."

"Perfect. Shall we begin?"

APPENDIX

'Since a man comes into this world through no fault of his own, since he is manifestly a joint inheritor of the accumulations of the past, and since those accumulations are more than sufficient to justify the claims that are here made for him, it follows:

(1) That every man without distinction of race, of color or professed belief or opinions, is entitled to the nourishment, covering, medical care and attention needed to realize his full possibilities of physical and mental development and to keep him in a state of health from his birth to death.

(2) That he is entitled to sufficient education to make him a useful and interested citizen, that special education should be so made available as to give him equality of opportunity for the development of his distinctive gifts in the service of mankind.

(3) That he may engage freely in any lawful occupation, earning such pay as the need for his work and the increment it makes to the common welfare may justify.

(4) That he shall have the right to buy or sell without any discriminatory restrictions anything which may be lawfully bought or sold.

(5) That he and his personal property lawfully acquired are entitled to police and legal protection from private violence, deprivation, compulsion, and intimidation.

(6) That he may move freely about the world at his own expense. That his private house or apartment or reasonably limited garden enclosure is his castle, which may be entered only with his consent.

(7) That a man unless he is declared by a competent authority to be a danger to himself and to others through mental abnormality, a declaration which must be annually confirmed, shall not be imprisoned for a more extended period than six days without being charged with a definite offense against the law, nor for more than three months without a public trial. At the end of the latter period, if he has not been tried

and sentenced by due process of law, he shall be released.

(8) That although a man is subject to the free criticism of his fellows, he shall have adequate protection from any lying or misrepresentation that may distress or injure him.

(9) That no man shall be subjected to any sort of mutilation or sterilization except with his own deliberate consent, freely given, nor to bodily assault, except in restraint of his own violence, nor to torture, beating or any other bodily punishment; he shall not be subjected to imprisonment with such an excess of silence, noise, light or darkness as to cause mental suffering, or to imprisonment in infected, verminous or otherwise insanitary quarters, or be put into the company of verminous or infectious people. He shall not be forced to take drugs nor shall they be administered to him without his knowledge and consent.

(10) That the provisions and principles embodied in this Declaration shall be more fully defined in a code of fundamental human rights which shall be made easily accessible to everyone.'

The New World Order- by H.G Wells 1940.

DANGERS OF ATMOSPHERIC ENTRY

The steep angle of friction burned red-hot against the bottom of the NASA command module. Traveling at 24,000 miles per hour increased the burn and turned the metal white-hot. The three astronauts inside gripped the handrails of their seats with remarkable strength, remaining solid and undeterred by the violent movements of the craft.

The walls of the craft contorted and stretched, poised to rip open like a can of sardines. The straining noise of metal panels was loud and should have overloaded the senses within the astronauts' heads, causing dizziness and confusion. But they remained still, heads up and backs straight. Their training had been vital for this mission.

On the underside of the craft, the heat shield reached 3,000 degrees, creating a cloud of plasma.

The astronauts were hit with the full force of seven Gs pulling on their bodies; this caused their grips on the handrail to loosen slightly, but none of them blacked out.

Three loud explosions marked deployment of the giant parachutes. As ropes tightened against the slack, the ship violently jolted upward before beginning its eerie, silent float toward the shimmering blue expanse below. Within moments, the craft slammed into the water as the parachutes dreamily floated down and rode the large waves caused by the craft's landing.

In the distance, large and small navy ships approached the craft as it bobbed in the water.

Finally, the USS Proteus reached the craft, and a small boat occupied by four men in dark blue radiation suits made their way to the spacecraft. The men attached chains to the command module and hoisted it out of the water. The parachutes hung as water poured from them.

A crane lowered the spacecraft onto the deck of the ship. Sailors applauded and roared in unison, like fans at a baseball-game.

Soon, the three astronauts shuffled into a large yellow and green containment booth. Like a car wash, jets of water shoot toward the astronauts, drenching them in disinfectant before washing their suits and helmets.

***

Five hundred miles to the west, in the Control Room at NASA, people celebrated with loud music and joyful laughter. The staff danced and drank champagne from little plastic cups, while confetti fell like snow, covering the carpeted floor.

This was a historical event for space exploration. Man had finally landed on the Moon and returned safely to Earth. Scientists would spend years analyzing the data and samples found on the Moon, exploring the unknown, and even searching for evidence of life on other planets.

Dr. Lilly Mcintosh sat in the far end of the room away from her colleagues, ignoring the revelries behind her and batting away the odd rogue balloon.

She peered at her computer screen and punched a few buttons on the keyboard to change the screen from a black and white fuzz to an image of the Moon's surface. The video feed from the module's exterior cameras had been lost in static interference, and she leaned forward, eager to see the events of the last thirty-six hours.

Lilly's eyes grew larger, bulging in shock as she witnessed the three astronauts being stalked by three strange creatures. Her jaw dropped as she focused intently, horrified, as the green humanoid creatures approached the NASA astronauts and pulled out a weapon that caused the men to collapse.

After a blip, the angle changed slightly to display another camera's feed. On the rocky surface of the Moon lay three lifeless bodies wearing NASA jumpsuits.

Lilly gasped incredulously and covered her mouth. If the astronauts' bodies were on the Moon, who just landed in the Pacific Ocean?

***

The USS Proteus floated quietly on the water as waves gently lapped against her large hull. The drone of the diesel engines had stopped. Seagulls circled above, squawking, while a few rested on the wires and poles crisscrossing the ship's deck, but there were no deckhands or sailors. The excitement aboard the vessel three hour earlier had vanished, as if this was a different ship.

A metal hatch creaked open and a humanoid creature stepped out. Its moist skin glistened in the sun, highlighting contours of muscular green limbs. It's clawed feet clinked across the metal deck, leaving a trail of slime.

Another creature, the smaller of the two, wearing the lower part of a NASA spacesuit and boots, emerged through the same hatch.

The smaller alien's head jerked to the left as it noticed movement in the corner of the deck. A sailor hiding behind some equipment sprang up and made a break for a nearby hatch. It was a pathetic attempt at escape.

With a flash of brilliant speed, the green creature pounced. It grabbed the sailor killing him instantly and then haphazardly launched the floppy body overboard.

The alien creature laid down with its back against the decking. The other alien knelt beside the prone one and, using his talon like a surgeon's scalpel, slowly opened the chest of his comrade.

He peeled back the skin and bones of the creature, and the body cracked and ripped as if attacked by a lion tearing its prey. At last, he exposed an illuminated purple circle. The alien closed his eyes, and the purple circle glowed brighter until it emitted a powerful beam of light into the sky. The beam hummed, sounding like electrical current pulsing through a machine.

On the bridge of the ship, the third alien rested his upturned arm on the control console. Various translucent wires connected his forearm to a computer terminal.

He closed his large black eyes, and suddenly a flood of yellow, purple, and blue light pulsed through the wires. Moments later, the computer displays at every station on the bridge turned to static.

***

Lilly frantically slid her chair back and got up. She headed straight for her boss, her lips tightened in annoyance as she had to dodge and weave through the throng of revelers. She tried to wave to get his attention, but Ted simply reciprocated the gesture, thinking she was joining in on the celebrations. It was hopeless.

When Lilly was steps away from her boss, all the computer displays blipped from their programs to static. Lilly stopped and stared at them, knowing something was wrong. Around her the partying continued.

She ran her hands through her hair and clenched her fists. Her head pounded and she could feel a pain behind her eyes. A migraine was brewing.

There had to be aliens aboard the USS Proteus. It was the only explanation for the malfunction of the monitoring equipment. NASA and the government were blind with no radar, no satellite, and zero communication link to the naval vessel. With no data feed of the upper atmosphere, the Earth was exposed and naked.

This could only mean one thing to Lilly: an alien assault against Earth.

***

A ship orbited far out in space at the edge of the Milky Way. A beam of purple light cut through the clouds and Earth's atmosphere, beaming through space to connect with the ship.

Aboard the spaceship, a large green humanoid creature sat, resting his clawed hands on the arms of his throne-like chair, The perch made him look powerful and majestic.

Chatter and movement filled the room as creatures scurried back and forth to each other and their computer displays. A general approached the leader, leaned in, and whispered something.

The leader stood, causing his minions to halt their activities and stare at him with bated breath. The room went silent.

"Zork zanch zala. Azora zachi."

Rough translation: "Our spies have made contact. Begin the attack."

ATTACK THEM FIRST

"Unfortunately, their ships have been detected on the outer rim of the galaxy," Captain Stammer said disappointingly, flattening his lips.

A member of the committee stood up, eyes fixed on the captain. "Are we to assume they will attack us?"

"It seems that way. They have decimated every other planet thus far."

The chambers erupted in loud, muddled chatter. Concerned faces filled the gallery.

"How long do you think we have before they are here?" another official said, panic evident in his aged trembling voice.

Before the captain could answer, Milo stood up sharply, the legs of his chair scraping across the floor behind him. He slammed his hand down on the bench in front of him causing a loud thud, the noise reverberated high into the cathedral ceiling of the building The room went silent as all eyes fell on him.

"This is why we needed to be prepared. I warned you all," he said, scanning the room with his finger, "we needed to attack them first." His pointed hand morphed into a fist.

"Sit down, Milo! We are well aware of what your feelings were." Fired back Travis, a senior member of the committee.

"I will not sit down," Milo said, and frowned. "You were the very one that told us violence was not the answer!" He clenched his teeth like a hungry lion ready to attack.

Whispers began to fill the room as the other members leaned into each other and spoke among themselves. Some nodded in agreement, others shook their heads.

"Do you still believe that?!" Milo demanded, pointing his accusatory finger at Travis. "You, with your peaceable approach, latitude, and kindness," he scoffed at the words, "now look where it got us. We need to leave our home, or be annihilated!"

"Please, please." Captain Stammer interrupted, raising his hands in hopes of calming the committee. Medals blazed across the lapel of his jacket. Each one had a story to tell. "Regardless of what should have been done or not done, we still need to evacuate. The starships are fueled and ready for take off. We have two weeks to load everyone onto the ships. This is our last chance of survival. We must reach the safety of the hidden galaxy."

"Or ..." Milo said slowly, drawing the word out in hopes of creating imagination in the minds of the unimaginable.

"Or what?" said the captain tilting his head in puzzlement.

"Or we stand our ground and FIGHT!" Milo's voice raised to a crescendo.

Captain Stammer's broad shoulders slumped. He let out an exhausted sigh. "We simply don't have the weaponry to defeat them. Their fusion capabilities far exceed our own."

Travis worked his way around the plenary chamber as seated officials shuffled forward to let him pass. He stepped onto the floor and stood facing the committee.

"Today, I implore all of you to think of your families and future generations. We have come face-to-face with the most brutal species—one that is driven by a lust for power and dominance. They will not take prisoners or slaves. We have seen them wipe out other civilizations that tried to defend themselves." His face reddened as he clenched his fists. "They have assumed the title of supreme ones, a natural species, and that all others are inferior. They wish to eradicate anyone that is not of their own race." He paced the floor, looking at each committee member, his brow furrowed with sadness and concern.

Many of the members nodded in unison, agreeing with Travis.

Milo waved dismissively and then crossed his arms. "I say we fight them!"

"Milo, I have warned you!" Travis growled, "for the sake of all the inhabitants of this planet, under law 4.7.5 section 3B, and as a senior member of this committee, I move to expel Milo Trinket from his position."

"How dare you! I call section 3C and demand a vote!" Milo puffed out his chest with an expression of arrogance, his lips curled defiantly, unwilling to concede.

The members of the committee pressed the electronic displays that lay in front of them. It took some time as members discussed matters among themselves. Finally, the voting was complete and the verdict was sealed.

An assistant to the committee stood up. He held a small flat computer screen in the palm of his hand that projected some numbers in 3D. The numbers were a few inches above the screen. Only the person holding the device could see the readout clearly.

"Well, what's the verdict?!" Milo said impatiently.

The assistant hesitated, his voice shaking. "According to Law 4.7.5 Section 3C, as a rebuttal to section 3B, all members have voted," he paused and glanced at Milo and nervously looked back at the readout, "Mr. Milo Trinket will relinquish all duties of this committee."

"Captain Stammer, remove Mr. Trinket from these chambers," Travis said commandingly.

"You're all fools!" Milo screamed, shaking his fists. Two guards grabbed him.

"You're going to allow these violent humans to invade our planet, our home?! You should all be ashamed of yourselves. I'm embarrassed to be a Sartinian!"

The end

ABOUT THE AUTHOR

Robbie Sheerin's love for storytelling has always been strong. For many years the Scottish writer from Oban has written short stories and essays. He is influenced by the founding fathers of classic sci-fi; Asimov, Heinlein, Bradbury, Serling, Clarke, and HG Wells, discovering escapism and imagination in their many works.

Evidence of his writing abilities was soon realized in 2020, when he published his stories and essays in various online and paperback journals. And so, the goal of publishing a book became possible for the self-taught writer. In 2021 a collection of his best sci-fi short stories were compiled.

Inspired by *The Twilight Zone* and *The Outer Limits*, he has always been drawn to the twists and turns of storytelling. His style of writing implements smoke and mirrors, which often catch readers off guard with strange and climactic endings.

Robbie is 42 years old and works as a quality inspector for a manufacturing company in Massachusetts, USA. He is married with one daughter, Lilly, and a cat and dog. He writes in his spare time.

"Write down your imagination"- Robbie Sheerin

A Word From The Author

If you enjoyed these stories and would like to see further publications and projects from Robbie and Silly Lilly Publishing, please write a review online for *Tales From Another Dimension*, and spread the news on social media. Reviews are how we thank writers, even if they are only a few words. This type of feedback also improves writers.

And finally, always keep an eye on your neighbors, they might just be from another dimension!!

Robbie Sheerin

Over and out!

For future transmissions for outer space login to

Www.talesfromanotherdimension.com

Made in the USA
Monee, IL
26 December 2021

87121761R00083